A Most Naked Solution

Also by Anna Randol

A Secret in Her Kiss

Coming Soon
Sins of a Virgin

A MOST NAKED SOLUTION

A Novella

ANNA RANDOL

AVONIMPULSE
An Imprint of HarperCollinsPublishers

Excerpt from *A Secret in Her Kiss* copyright © 2012 by Anna Clevenger.

Excerpt from *Sins of a Virgin* copyright © 2012 by Anna Clevenger.

EPub Edition JULY 2012 ISBN: 9780062121721

Print Edition ISBN: 9780062121738

10 9 8 7 6 5 4 3 2 1

A MOST NAKED SOLUTION

Chapter One

Weltford, England
1816

Lord Camden Grey glared at the ink-spotted paper in front of him. Damnation. Was that a six or an eight? Perhaps a three? He placed his quill back in the ink and pressed the heels of his hands against his bleary eyes.

He should have stopped working on the equation hours ago, but the solution had seemed so close this time. If only he'd worked a little harder or faster, perhaps he'd have been able to—

A knock again sounded on his door, reminding him what had startled him into splashing ink everywhere in the first place.

"Yes?" He knew his tone was harsher than it should have been, but he hadn't slept in—he checked the clock—twenty hours, and his servants knew better than to disturb him. If that fool Ipswith found an answer first, Camden would never again be able to set foot in the Royal Mathematical Society. The chairman, his father, would see to it. Just as he had seen to convincing Ipswith to research the exact same theorem to put Camden in his place.

The door opened and Rafferty entered, his stoic butler façade remaining in place despite the crumpled papers littering the carpet at his feet. "There is a . . . man to see you, sir." There was a significant distaste in his pronunciation of the word *man*.

Camden raised his brow. What was he then, a goat? Really, it was no wonder he found conversing such a waste. It was an imprecise medium. "What is his business?"

"He wishes to speak to the justice of the peace."

Camden glanced at the clock. "At three in the morning? Has there been a death?"

Rafferty cleared his throat and didn't make eye contact. "It is three in the afternoon, sir."

Camden swiveled to stare at the drawn curtains behind him. Indeed. Amend that—he'd been awake for thirty-two hours instead of twenty. Exhaustion hit him like a blow to the side of his head. He scrubbed at the grit in his eyes. "Did he say if it was urgent?"

As impressive as the title of justice of the peace sounded, it usually only amounted to settling squabbles about sheep and stolen chamber pots. He wouldn't have accepted the appointment to the position at all had there been any other men who met the requirements in Weltford, save drunk-off-his-arse Stanfield.

"The fellow claims to have information on the Harding death, sir."

That would be worth delaying sleep. "Where did you put him?"

"In the library, sir."

Camden stood, twisting side to side briefly to loosen the knots in his back, then strode past his butler and down the stairs.

He smelled his guest before he saw him. The air in the corridor stank of stale onions and spoiled ale. And he wasn't even in the same room yet.

Camden stepped into the library, then silently groaned when he saw his guest. "Mr. Spat?" Lloyd Spat, less than affectionately known about the village as Tubs, sat in the center of the room, his enormous girth filling the settee from arm to arm.

"Ah, Lord Grey! A pleasure to see you. A real pleasure." He tried to struggle to his feet but gave up after a single attempt. "There were a reward for information on the death of Lord Harding? A sizable one?"

"If your information proves to be of use." But he'd offered the money over three months ago at the death of Viscount Harding. While he still found it difficult to believe the death resulted from of a poacher's bullet, he found it even more unlikely that Tubs wouldn't have claimed the reward if he had real information. The man would do anything for his next pint. "Why wait to come forward?"

"Well, I feared for my life. Near trembled at the thought of what would happen to me if they found out I spoke."

"If who found out?" Camden focused on breathing through his mouth.

"The men."

He was too tired for this. His only hope was a strictly linear line of questioning. Camden spun the standing globe next to him absently, tapping every third line of longitude. He returned to the original question. "Why tell me now?"

"Well you might ask, sir. Mr. Haws, that greedy old bastard, has decided that my word is no longer good enough for him. He says if I'm wanting another drop of ale from his tavern, he needs to be seeing some of the coin he's owed. Now I'm rightly offended at such rudeness and I have a mind to take my business to another tavern, but my health's no longer what it were. And I needs to be close to my lodgings and my dear Mrs. Spat."

So his next drink was worth more than information that might cost him his life. That logic would have been too much on a day when fully awake; Camden stood no chance of sorting it out now.

Tubs rubbed his hands together, then glanced nervously about the room. "No one will find out the news came from me, right?"

"Not unless you tell them."

Tubs nodded, his chin disappearing into the rippling folds at his neck. "Well, then. The day after the murder I were at the tavern."

Camden had never seen him anywhere but at the tavern.

"I were sitting at my table in the corner when I hears voices behind me. It were two blokes discussing getting paid. Now I normally keeps to my own business but one of the gents says, 'The deed is done?' Now I know that when men are talking about deeds, that's not something that I needs to be hearing, but I were right there so I couldn't not hear them."

Camden stopped spinning the globe, his hand coming to rest somewhere in Russia. Tubs finally had his full attention.

It wasn't Camden's responsibility as justice of the peace to investigate crimes, only to rule on small squabbles, or for more serious matters, to decide if there was enough evidence for a criminal to be sent on to the formal court. While he gave the cases his full attention, he'd never been tempted to become involved past his limited role. It was the responsibility of the victim or his family to prosecute the crime.

But something about the Harding case had seemed suspicious. Camden had finally ruled with the coroner's jury because he'd had no evidence to contradict the theory of the poacher's bullet, but it had always seemed too convenient. As if someone had decided three plus three equaled five because they didn't want to be bothered to count to six.

Then the widow's powerful family had swooped in to ensure the whole matter stayed quiet. Her father and her brothers stayed at her side, keeping her distant from everyone. Lady Harding's father—the Earl of Riverton, himself—had visited Camden to ask for discretion when dealing with the case.

Camden had agreed because he knew better than to deny a powerful man like the earl without cause. He also knew the earl's oldest son, Darton, and he trusted him.

To a point.

But the whole situation had made him wary. More alert. He'd asked a few questions about town but had come up empty.

Tubs cracked his knuckles, the popping interspersing his words. "Then the other fellow says, 'He fell like a sack of turnips. Easiest job I've ever done.' Then he laughed. Now I hadn't heard about the good viscount's death yet, but something in his voice made my skin fair crawl off my body."

"Did you get a good look at either of the men?"

Tubs's eyes bulged. "There's no way I were going to let them know I'd heard them. What with them being hired killers."

Camden could hear his own teeth grinding. "Then what information do you have that you think will earn you the reward?"

"Well, then they started talking about returning to London." He looked hopeful at this bit of information, then sighed when Camden didn't react. "Then one of the fellows said, 'Did you collect the rest of the blunt from her?'"

Camden stepped away from the globe. "Her?" Why had an image of Lady Harding appeared in his mind?

"That's what he said as clear as day."

"Did they give a name? Anything more specific?" Camden tried to think of what he knew of Lady Harding, but came up with little. Oh, he could picture her clearly enough, the pretty young woman who'd lingered outside her brother's mathematics lessons when Camden had gone to tutor him almost seven years ago. The slender, delicate grace of her body and the almost elfin point of her chin. He'd liked knowing that she hid in the corridor to hear his lessons. But he hadn't spoken but the merest greetings to her.

Then the Hardings had been at their house in Weltford only rarely. He couldn't remember if he'd ever been invited to an event at Harding House. He paid little attention to the social engagements in the area.

And if he were completely honest with himself, he'd had no desire to see the girl who'd written him the only letter he'd received while in the army—a love letter—with another man.

Tubs grunted and tugged on his ear. "No. They left right quick after that."

Camden had little proof that Lady Harding was the woman that the killers referred to. Except, why hadn't she or her family done more to find the shooter? Why had she been content with the coroner's ruling? Why had her family been so intent on keeping him away from her? They'd claimed her prostrate with grief. All his questions had gone through her father.

"Do I get the money?" Tubs asked.

"Only if your information proves to be correct." Despite his own suspicions, he had no proof that Tubs's story was true.

"But I took time away from my dear wife to come to help with your investigation."

Frowning, Camden tossed him a guinea. "For your trouble. But you get no more unless your information leads to an arrest."

The money disappeared into Tubs's pocket. "It will, sir. Everything I told you is as true as my name."

Tubs lumbered to his feet and Rafferty escorted him out.

Camden had planned to pay his respects to Lady Harding at some point, perhaps see what manner of woman she'd matured into. Now it appeared he had no choice.

She may have grown up to be a murderer.

"You want me to give away all of the books in the library?" Lady Sophia Harding's housekeeper's mouth opened then snapped closed. "But, my lady, the books must be worth hundreds of pounds."

Eight hundred and sixty-three pounds, to be precise.

Sophia knew. She'd purchased every one of them when they'd renovated the house last year.

Now the gilded leather spines sickened her.

She took a deep breath. "Yes, every one of them."

"What will you put in here instead, my lady?" Mrs. Gilray asked.

Sophia smiled. She had absolutely no idea. She would pick what she liked. She didn't even know what that would be. Perhaps piles of penny dreadfuls or scandalous novels. More books on mathematics. Treatises on the best way to grow peas.

All she knew was that no one would have a say in it but her.

She wouldn't fret over her choices, thinking and rethinking each one. Trying to pick those Richard would approve of while knowing she'd never be able to guess correctly.

Richard was dead.

And now she intended to reclaim the library from his influence. Sophia traced a finger down the edge of one of the books. If only it were as easy to reclaim herself. "Send them to St. Wilfred's orphanage."

"Very good, my lady." Mrs. Gilray was too new to dare question her.

Sophia turned at the sound of heavy boots in the corridor. Her eyes widened at the sight of her head gardener.

Mud caked Wicken's boots and his white hair jutted out from his head in awkward clumps. "There's an urgent matter I must discuss with you regarding the *rose gardens*."

Sophia tried to smile as if urgent meetings about greenery

were a normal occurrence, but her mind was racing. "That will be all, Mrs. Gilray."

Mrs. Gilray's fascinated gaze swung back and forth between the other two occupants of the room, but she bobbed a curtsey and glided from the library.

Wicken closed the door behind her with a click, the kindly lines on his face deep with worry. "Sorry, my lady. I know this is most unusual. But I thought it important that you know."

Sophia swallowed against sudden unease. "Is something amiss?"

"My daughter just sent word from the village. The justice of the peace has been asking questions about your husband's death."

"What questions?"

He rubbed his right arm, the arm her husband had broken when Wicken refused to tell Richard where she was hiding.

Sophia fought not to stare, not to choke on the guilt that burned in her chest at the stiff way the arm hung at his side.

"What enemies Harding might have had. Same as he did right after the death."

"Has anyone said anything?"

"Not as far as I know, but it's only a matter of time before one of the villagers lets something slip."

Sophia's hands clenched into fists at her sides. Lord Grey wouldn't find anything. She wouldn't allow it. Not when that might lead him directly to her husband's killer—her father.

Chapter Two

Lord Grey tapped his hand on the well-polished bar. "I thought you said you'd have time to speak to me this morning, Haws."

The barkeep shrugged and glanced at his wife, who'd just bustled in with a tray. "Sorry. Perhaps in a few days. I find myself right busy today."

Camden glanced at the near-empty tavern from the corner of his eye.

"I don't want you to have come all this way for nothing, though," Mrs. Haws said with a smile. She placed a steaming meat pie in front him. "Please enjoy. It's my treat."

Even though Camden's stomach rumbled at the savory aroma, he stared at the two of them. "So you don't remember two strangers in the tavern around the time of Lord Harding's death?"

Haws glanced at his wife and she answered, her rosy apple cheeks stretched into a friendly smile. "Can't say I rightly do. Believe it or not, we get a fair number of travelers through here. I can't remember anyone in particular from so long ago. Now eat your pie."

Camden had only moved to this village two years ago after being granted his barony, but that didn't stop Mrs. Haws from treating him like she'd known him since he was a boy. It was almost enough to make him move to another county. He picked up his fork and took a bite of the pie, hoping his motion would cover the unease caused by maternal regard. He almost groaned as the flakey crust crumbled on his tongue, revealing the thick, beefy gravy. But as good as the food was, it couldn't distract him—at least not for long—from the suspicion that something was amiss.

"I'll have to have a word with your cook about getting a proper meal in you. Sweet mercy, Lottie!" She turned her attention to the maid who'd just sloshed half her bucket of water on the floor. "Pay attention to your work, dear. Not to Lord Grey."

The maid blushed and ducked her head as she scurried away. When she returned, she had a lad of about thirteen at her side helping her.

After Camden finished his pie and moved on to being ignored by the blacksmith and then the owner of the livery stable, he was certain something was wrong. The thin man returned to grooming his horses, studiously ignoring Camden's presence.

Eventually, he found himself in the middle of the village square leaning against the trunk of a gnarled oak. Perhaps he should speak with the tree. He'd probably have a greater chance of getting answers from it than from the villagers.

"They aren't going to talk to you."

Camden turned toward the brittle female voice and saw a pinched-faced woman in black. Her mousy brown hair had been scraped back into a bun so tight it should have done something to lessen the bitter creases around her mouth and eyes. "Why is that?"

"Because she was here."

Camden was becoming rather annoyed with ambiguous pronouns. "Who?"

"Lady Harding. She was here earlier, sneaking about. I'm sure she warned everyone not to talk to you."

The woman looked vaguely familiar. Camden finally placed her. "You're her housekeeper, are you not? Mrs. Ovard?"

Mrs. Ovard's lips thinned. "Not any longer. She let me go. As if I hadn't worked in that house for thirty years."

"Why did she let you go?"

"Because I knew her for what she was. She isn't the good Christian woman she pretends to be. She hated her husband. She wasted no time disposing of his things after he was killed."

Camden shifted away from the tree, hands tensing at his sides. "Do you think she had something to do with his death?"

The woman's nostrils flared. "Why else would she be creeping about, warning people not to speak with you?"

Camden knew that there was undoubtedly more to this woman's motivation than she'd admit to. Revenge being a likely one. But he couldn't disregard her accusations. Especially when they fit perfectly with his suspicions.

"Did you observe anything unusual in Lady Harding's behavior around the time her husband was killed?"

"She purchased a pistol. One of the maids told me she saw it in the room."

"Eugena Ovard!" Mrs. Haws trundled out of the tavern, a rolling pin brandished in her hand. "You had better not be tattling any of your filth in that young man's ears."

Mrs. Ovard ducked behind him. "I'm only telling him God's own truth."

"Well, I imagine the good Lord will have a thing or two to say about your *truth* when you meet him."

"It's better than lying for a trollop." Mrs. Ovard stiffened her spine and stalked away.

Mrs. Haws tapped the rolling pin against her hand, dislodging a puff of flour. "She's a bitter woman. I wouldn't believe a word she says, my lord."

Whom did he trust? The bitter woman or the lying one? Damnation, this is what he got for becoming involved. As contrary as his equations might be, at least he knew what to do with them. "Did Lady Harding ask you not to speak with me?"

Mrs. Haws focused on dusting flour off her apron. "No."

"But she did speak to you this morning?"

The woman's cheeks darkened. "She might have stopped by for a quick chat and a piece of pie."

"What did you chat about?"

"Really, it isn't my place to speak about my betters. Perhaps you should go speak to Lady Harding. You'll know right away that she hasn't a thing to hide." The woman clutched the rolling pin tightly to her ample bosom.

Camden nodded. He intended to do just that.

CHAPTER THREE

"I can tell him you are not at home, my lady," her butler said.

Sophia straightened her skirts with a quick tug. She wanted to hide. She wanted to run to where Lord Grey wouldn't be able to follow.

But she glared at the pale, frightened woman reflected in the mirror, willing her to disappear. She wasn't that woman anymore.

Yes, you are, a small voice inside her mocked. *You are a coward. You will always be a coward. If you weren't a coward, your father wouldn't have had to come clean up the mess you made of your life.*

But she'd been about to clean it up. Her husband had just been killed before she could. She would have done it this time. She would have stood up to Richard—no matter the beating it earned her—and then left him.

Like the dozen other times you made that resolve?

Sophia shut out the voice as she walked down the stairs. No matter how cowardly she'd behaved, she refused to let any blame fall on her father.

Sophia slowed as she neared the parlor where Lord Grey waited. Why now? Why after all these months was he finally investigating?

Lord Grey stood by the window. Her husband, Richard, would have looked like an angel standing in that pool of light. His golden ringlets would have sparkled, his eyes would have been as light as the summer sky. Ladies would have sighed over his beauty.

Lord Grey was the opposite; rather than radiating the light, he seemed to absorb it, the sun's rays disappearing into his short dark hair. His jaw was too strong and his brows too harsh. A generous woman, or a confused young girl, might call his face striking. His body, as well, was too strong, too broad, too hard to ever be called as paltry a word as *beautiful*.

The forgotten pleasure of a girlhood infatuation fluttered through her. He'd come to her home for a few months after her brother Darton had fallen ill with inflammation of the lungs and had to be sent home from Oxford. Mr. Grey had been a fellow student trying to earn enough money to continue his schooling.

Sophia had hidden in the corridor so she could listen to the low rumble of his voice, catch a glimpse of the shape of his lips from the shadows. Eventually, even the mathematics he spoke of fascinated her.

He'd never said more than good morning to her, but her young girlish heart had liked to think he knew she lingered outside the door, and spoke extra loudly so she could hear the lessons.

And one time when she'd been feeling particularly daring, she'd placed her completed version of an assignment he'd given her brother on his desk. She'd found the corrected paper placed in her usual spot in the corridor the next day.

As Lord Grey turned away from the window, the memory faded, a deeper, more feminine appreciation taking root. She'd thought such emotions had been crushed beyond redemption by Richard. Perhaps she'd been mistaken.

Yet there was a coldness in Lord Grey that kept her from examining the sensation too closely. New lines about his eyes that she didn't remember. A cynical twist of his mouth. As much as she'd swooned over the more youthful version of the man in front of her, she knew nothing of him now.

"Can I help you?" She kept her voice soft and musical, her gaze submissive. If there was one thing she'd learned from Richard, it was how to appease a man.

"Lady Harding." As he bowed, his gaze swept her. Her heart hammered as he studied her like she'd always wished he would.

Except now she didn't want his scrutiny.

"Who wanted your husband dead?"

His bluntness surprised her. Although it shouldn't have. "I am well. Thank you."

Lord Grey's lips tightened as his breech of etiquette was pointed out. "This is not a social call."

"No, I learned long ago that you only give attention when it suits you." A blush heated her cheeks. She thought she'd gotten over never receiving a response to the letter she'd sent him as a girl. Apparently not entirely.

Lord Grey folded his arms across his chest. "Did you kill him?"

She wished for a moment that her brother Bennett hadn't

returned to Constantinople. His hulking presence behind her would have been nice, but she banished that thought. Allowing others to take care of her problems had tangled her in this mess in the first place.

"No. And I do not know who did." She should offer him a seat, pour him a drink, but her sudden spurt of defiance kept her silent. It felt so fragile—so seductive—that she let him stand. She'd analyzed every part of her soul over the past few months, trying to decide which bits to keep and which parts she could no longer tolerate.

This defiance she'd definitely keep.

His lips thinned. "Did your husband have enemies?"

Sophia opened her mouth to tell him the truth about the kind of man her husband had been. "No, he was quite well liked."

Curse it all. Why did her rebellion fail her now? But the lie was rooted too deep to be pulled out with a single effort.

And if she told Lord Grey what type of man her husband had been, then he'd wonder what type of weakling allowed herself to remain with such a man. Of all the things he could think of her, she refused to let Lord Grey think her weak.

He stalked toward her. "Did you like your husband, Lady Harding?"

Sophia lifted her chin. He couldn't expect her to answer that. "Why are you here, Lord Grey? My husband has been dead for more than three months. Surely, the time to investigate has passed."

"You've done little to find your husband's killer."

The bluntness again. "The coroner's jury ruled it a poacher."

He stopped so close that the toes of his boots touched the hem of her skirts. His eyes were as dark as twice-brewed coffee. "I received new information on the killer."

Sophia held her ground even as every instinct told her to flee. She sucked in a deep breath, drawing in air despite the ice encasing her chest. She supposed she should summon surprise or excitement, but at this point, she was more concerned about hiding her terror. "What information?"

"You don't sound very happy, Lady Harding."

"I find myself stunned. I apologize if my reaction shocks you. But then I'd remind you, sir, that you know me not at all."

Lord Grey stepped back, his eyes narrowed. "You are right. I do not know you, and therefore, I have no reason to trust you."

"And that makes you *distrust* me?"

"Evidence makes me distrust you, Lady Harding."

"What evidence?"

Lord Grey was silent a moment. "A witness saw two men discussing the murder in the tavern."

Oh, no. Her father and oldest brother, Darton. Had they really allowed themselves to be seen? She shouldn't have allowed them to come. She should have denied her husband's abuse for a little longer. "Which two men?"

"The witness was rather vague on the details. But I was hoping you could tell me. Did you hire them?"

Sophia rested her hand briefly on the back of a chair, using it to keep herself upright. He didn't know, then. She still had a chance to keep him from finding out. "No. I believe

I already made that clear. I'm sorry I cannot be of more help."

He smiled slightly. "But you can."

Sophia stilled at the dark promise in his voice.

"Some people in the village seem to be of the opinion that you don't want them to speak to me."

She tried to step around him, but he blocked her.

"I suppose that is all a misunderstanding, is it not? You'll have no problem accompanying me and letting the townspeople know that you want them to cooperate fully?"

"Of course, I'll go." If she was by his side, she could control what he knew.

Lord Grey offered her his arm. "My carriage is outside."

She hesitated only a second before taking it, reluctant to touch him. She hadn't touched a man since her husband died. Not her father. Not any of her brothers. Yet as her fingers came to rest on the hard column of his forearm, she found it disturbingly pleasant. He smelled of soap and parchment, familiar smells, as if nothing had changed in the years since she'd last seen him.

But everything had changed. She was no longer an innocent young girl and he was no longer a young man she fancied from afar.

He thought her a liar at best and a murderer at worst. Not the basis for respectful, healthy interaction.

Her butler handed her a bonnet and pelisse and opened the front door. She stepped outside into the sunshine.

A gunshot cracked.

Pulling her to his chest, Lord Grey drove them both to the ground. All the air rushed out of her chest in a pained grunt as his weight landed on her. Her bonnet and cloak twisted in an awkward pile under her back as her face pressed against his waistcoat.

"Go! Secure the perimeter." Lord Grey's shouted order rumbled through his chest.

Thumps reverberated through the stone as footsteps—she assumed belonging to her butler and footmen—ran past.

Had Lord Grey been shot? She tried to ask but couldn't get enough air to speak. She struggled against his chest.

He rolled off her and rose to his feet. Before she could refill her lungs, he'd scooped her up, carried her inside, and set her on the floor of the entry hall away from windows.

Wicken ran inside and pulled the doors closed, his face flushed, his hair wild. "Are you injured, my lady?"

Camden grabbed him by the collar. "I assume you trust this man?"

She nodded, not yet capable of speech. She stared at a space between the tiles on the floor until her panic bent to her will, slipping away. Terror did her no good. It only made her attacker stronger, the fists faster and kicks harder. Calm might not stop the pain, but it let her control it. Or at least some of it.

Camden released her gardener. "Guard the door." He strode toward the windows, positioning himself so he could see out but not be seen.

Wicken braced himself against the front door. "Former Fifty-Third Foot. Served in the colonies. You were a military man, too, weren't you?"

"Captain, Royal Engineers."

Sophia started to stand, but Lord Grey planted his hand on her shoulder. "Someone shot at your head with a rifle. Do not present them with a second chance."

She gasped as her sore backside connected with the floor.

Immediately, Camden dropped into a crouch next to her. "You *are* injured." His hands skimmed down her arms. "Anything broken?"

She caught his hand before he continued down her legs. His touch had been light and impersonal, yet sensation shimmered over her skin. "I'm just a bit sore."

The tingling must have affected her alone because Lord Grey had already redirected his attention through the window.

Sophia fought for calm again, the awareness along her arms interfering. But she scooted until she was against the wall, then stood.

Camden glowered at her over his shoulder. "Sit."

"My servants are at risk. I'm not going to sit cowering on the floor."

"Stay behind me then." He glared one final time, but shifted so she could see past him.

She tried to keep her focus on the footmen attacking Wicken's perfectly trimmed hedges, not on the circle of sunshine that fell on the smooth wool of Camden's sleeve, leaving it warm when it brushed her cheek as she peered past.

After several long minutes, the footmen trudged back toward the house. Empty-handed.

Lord Grey swore.

"You're in the presence of a lady," Wicken reminded him.

Glancing back, Camden managed to look both abashed and annoyed. She thought perhaps his ears darkened. "I beg your pardon, Lady Harding."

She could hardly take offense at him uttering the same words she'd been thinking. "You know Darton. Nothing you say could shock me."

The harsh lines on his face softened. "Is that a challenge?"

Heavens, that sounded like flirtation. Sophia was so stunned the only thing she could do was stand there like a ninny.

Whatever caused that was definitely not an aspect of her character she wanted to keep.

His tension returned, deepening the fine lines around his eyes. "Are you truly uninjured? I'm not precisely a feather-weight."

Sophia could suddenly recall with exact detail the contours of his hard body covering her. Protecting her. "I'm well. Thank you for your quick action."

He grunted in what she supposed was acceptance.

Wicken hurried to unlock the door as the butler and footmen returned. "I thought the danger to you gone, my lady."

Lord Grey spun toward her. "What danger?"

She cast a warning glance at her gardener, who looked suspiciously unrepentant.

"Nothing recent," she said.

Her butler and footmen entered and she quickly moved the focus to them. "Did you find anything?"

Her butler dusted a leaf from his jacket. "Nay, my lady. Only where the ball hit the doorframe."

None of the flushed faces held any answers. What was

going on? She had no enemies. Her money came from a trust her father had arranged as part of her dowry. It had been released to her last week after her husband's will was finally settled. Her husband's heir had dowered her this house out of the many he'd inherited because he hadn't wanted it. There were no hard feelings there.

"Perhaps I asked the wrong question earlier, Lady Harding," Lord Grey said. "Who wants *both* you and your husband dead?"

CHAPTER FOUR

Camden watched Lady Harding bite her lush lower lip, leaving it moist and rosy. "I cannot think of anyone."

Her spine was perfectly straight, her face serene. If it weren't for her teeth dragging over her lip, he would have thought her completely unmoved.

But he knew better. And he had to fight the urge to sweep her into his arms and away from danger.

Camden had always preferred vibrant women—dark brunettes, fiery redheads. Lady Harding was the antithesis of that. Pale skin, pale hair, a delicate rose tinting her cheeks. It should have been easy to overlook her. But instead he found himself drawn closer, like to a watercolor, desperate to take it all in and not miss one subtle detail.

If she was her husband's murderer, why had someone tried to kill *her*? And why now?

She was still hiding something. He'd caught that look she'd given her gardener.

He tore his attention away from her to the concerned faces of her servants, who had gathered about the hall. "Can anyone think of someone who might wish your mistress harm?"

All the servants except for Wicken shook their heads. Wicken rubbed the white stubble salting his chin. "His lordship had many a mistress. Some of them's the jealous type." He didn't flinch as Lady Harding and the other servants glared. "It's true and you all know it. I see no reason Lord Grey shouldn't know it as well. I never understood how lying about the type of man Lord Harding was did anyone any favors."

Lady Harding's face turned crimson, but she didn't refute the claim.

Camden wanted to shoot Lord Harding himself. Camden was a firm believer in fidelity. There was a symmetry there that appealed to him. If a man expected his wife to remain loyal then she had the right to expect the same. Harding had no right to have disgraced Sophia—Sophia? When had he begun to think of her that way?

Undoubtedly when she was soft and lithe beneath him on the ground.

"Anyone who might be violent?" Lord Grey asked.

The gardener looked disappointed, as if Camden had asked the wrong question. "None that I can think of."

Which brought him full circle. He needed to go the village and see if anyone remembered those men Tubs had seen and if anyone had noticed anything today.

He no longer wanted Sophia to come, yet he retained his initial confidence that people would only be willing to speak to him if Sophia ordered them to. And with her by his side, he could ensure she did.

CHAPTER FIVE

Lord Grey's carriage rattled over the bumpy dirt road. Since it only had the two seats for the passengers, each lurch pressed Sophia's leg against his thigh. Fortunately, he'd pulled out a page of numbers and letters from a folio under the seat and was studying them intently. He seemed unaware of the intimacy the carriage ride provoked.

The wind dragged dark clouds through the sky and rustled the leaves in the oak trees. She welcomed the cool on her cheeks.

Sophia watched the backs of the two grooms riding ahead of them as outriders. Was it wrong to hope someone *was* trying to kill her? If the same man had shot at her and Richard, then it wasn't her father.

She let the breeze dry her tears of relief. After all, she didn't yet know what was the truth.

Her father and brother Darton had visited her three months ago, anguished and enraged. They had received a letter from her brother Bennett, telling them of Richard's abuse. They demanded to know if it was true. And for the first time in her life she hadn't lied to them. Her stomach clenched as she remembered her father sinking, ashen-faced, to the floor, guilt contorting his face. He'd demanded that she leave. But she refused. She couldn't go yet—not because she hadn't wanted to, but because she had to confront Richard first. She'd planned to do it that night.

Her brother Bennett had whisked her away from Richard once before, and she'd been too weak in the face of Richard's anguished pleas. She'd gone back, unable to stop herself from trying to fix things one last time.

So when she'd told her father to wait for her in town, it was because she had to prove to herself that she was strong enough to leave on her own. Strong enough to walk out the door and not bend when Richard grew angry, or worse, when he wept and claimed he couldn't do without her. Strong enough not to fear his fists when she defied him.

Her father had sworn he'd put a bullet through Richard's head before letting him set foot in this house again.

Three hours later Richard was dead.

The carriage hit a rut, rattling her teeth so hard she bit her tongue. The taste of blood in her mouth was so familiar she didn't even wince.

So had she been wrong all along? Her father was a famed diplomat. He praised negotiation and reconciliation. But she'd never seen him enraged before. In fact, she'd never seen him even slightly angered.

Had she been too quick to think him a killer?

Sophia closed her eyes briefly, shivering in the chill as the clouds swallowed the sun.

The next rut drove her against Lord Grey's shoulder, fleetingly reminding her of the time she'd *accidentally* brushed against him as he'd hurried up to the schoolroom to teach her brother. She hadn't slept at all that night, trying to commit the feel of his arm to memory.

Apparently, she hadn't been as efficient as she'd thought. She didn't remember the thickness of his shoulder or the smooth slope of muscle. Or perhaps that was new?

She peered around his shoulder, trying to distract herself. "What are you studying?"

"I'm trying to find a formula for the roots of a fifth-degree polynomial equation in terms of the coefficients of the polynomial, using only the usual algebraic operations."

She liked how he left it at that, expecting her to understand.

Or perhaps he thought it too far beyond her and didn't want to be bothered to explain.

She watched him study the paper as they travelled, occasionally repeating a number aloud. Or shuffling to find another page to compare some equations. He often squinted and lifted a page closer to his face. After a few of these adjustments, he glanced at her from the corner of his eyes, then pulled a pair of spectacles from his pocket. He cleared his throat. "Some of the writing is hard to read." He cut another quick look at her again before slipping them on.

She could have told him he had no reason to fear her mockery. The spectacles only emphasized the masculine strength to his cheekbones and the keen brilliance in his eyes.

When his long finger slid along a column of numbers, she felt it along her spine. She needed a distraction from her distraction.

Who wanted her dead? That should be the real question occupying her thoughts. Richard had wooed dozens of mistresses and countless lovers, but he was dead. She couldn't imagine why one of them would be trying to kill her years later. And Richard had stripped one thing after another from her until she'd been left with nothing. No friends of her own. No enemies, either.

A disturbing thought occurred to her. "*You* don't have any enemies, do you, Lord Grey?"

"Hmm?" he asked, his attention on the paper.

"Do you have any enemies?"

He looked up, his mind obviously still elsewhere. She could see the exact moment when his concentration latched onto her, his gaze pinning her like a butterfly to cork.

"Enemies? No." But then he frowned. "At least none who know how to shoot a rifle." A grin flitted across this face. "Ipswith wouldn't know which end to point. I'm a mathematician, Lady Harding. We're not precisely known for our violent tendencies."

She'd seen his face as he watched for her attacker. She didn't doubt that he was capable of violence. "You were in the army."

He tucked the paper he'd been reading back into the folder. "As an engineer. And I'm by far the exception in the Royal Mathematical Society."

His arrogance reminded her so much of Darton that she couldn't help smiling. Heavens, she was half-amazed the poor, neglected muscles in her face even remembered what to do. "That's when you were awarded the barony, was it not?"

After his last comment, she hadn't expected him to be

able to look humble, but he did a very creditable job, dropping his gaze and clearing his throat. "Yes. Although, really, the entire company deserved the praise. I may have designed the bridge, but they were the ones who had to build it."

The bridge had saved the lives of half of Wellington's retreating army, if she remembered the story correctly. Then he'd helped hold off the French forces with rifle fire while the remaining few crossed.

"Surely there had to have been officers jealous of your fame."

Lord Grey shook his head. "Envy does indeed strike soldiers, but I was given the title five years ago. And I've remained fairly quiet since then."

"No angry lovers?" Where had that come from? Definitely not something she needed to know about.

He lifted a brow. "Lovers, yes. Angry, no. They tend to be rather satisfied."

As if she needed more thoughts of being satisfied by Lord Grey. She turned her face into the wind to cool the burning in her cheeks. "I'm trying to think of suspects."

All humor drained from his face. "The person intended to wound, if not kill you. Are you ready to be honest about what you know."

Camden wasn't sure what he expected her to say. He knew there was slim chance of her actually cooperating, so he almost missed the brief moment of indecision that flashed across her face.

Then she said, "Will you do the same?"

Camden frowned. "I'm not hiding anything." Except perhaps how oddly distracting he was finding her lips, but he was certain she didn't want to hear that fact.

"You think I had something to do with my husband's death."

He paused. "I'm not certain, but I do think it's possible. And I do know you are hiding something."

The carriage drew to a halt in front of the Dancing Pig tavern. Camden leapt down, then assisted Sophia onto the cobbles.

Only a few men dotted the taproom as they entered, Tubs being one of them. The guinea must have been enough to convince Haws to allow him access to the ale again. The maid, Lottie, stood next to him, collecting his empty tankard.

Haws shifted behind the bar, the rag in his hand slowing, wiping the same circle as they approached. "Lord Grey. Lady Harding. It's a surprise to see you both again. So soon."

"I've come to ask again if you remember any strangers from around the time of Lord Harding's murder. Lady Harding has come along to tell you how grateful she'll be for any help."

Sophia's smile was brittle. "Of course."

Haws slung the rag over his shoulder. "Well, er . . ."

Mrs. Haws exploded out of the kitchen. A look passed between her and Sophia. And Camden knew, in that instant, that his plan would be an utter failure. He'd learn nothing even if Sophia swore on the Bible that she wanted everyone to cooperate.

Yet ever obstinate, he tried one last time. "I know two men were here after the murder. Two men from London."

Sophia paled. Disappointment dropped into Camden's

gut, a painful, heavy thing. "You wouldn't know anything about two men from London?"

A ragged party of farmers entered the tavern and claimed a table by the window.

"I know many men from London, but not two who would have been in this tavern." Camden had to lean in close to hear Sophia's words, but even from a mile away he would have recognized her stubborn determination.

He lowered his voice. "Then why does this investigation frighten you? What are you hiding?"

"Nothing."

Camden barely registered the growl coming from his throat until Sophia backed away from him, eyes wary.

Good. Perhaps she'd rethink whatever foolishness was going on here.

Cold ale sloshed in his face. Camden choked, wiping at the liquid stinging his eyes and running down his chin. "What the devil?"

Haws shoved his cup-wielding wife from the room. "Sorry, sir. I have no idea—"

"I'll not have him scaring women in my tavern—"

Haws put his hand over her mouth. "Too much time in the hot kitchen. Lewis, get Lord Grey a towel. Lewis? Damn it all, where is that boy?"

The lad he'd seen yesterday skidded through the kitchen door, his blond curls hanging limply over his face. "Here." His voice cracked halfway through. He ducked past Haws and grabbed a clean cloth, tossing it toward Camden, his expression sullen.

Camden grabbed at the clean linen but missed. Sophia

retrieved it and pressed it into his hand, amusement lighting the blue of her eyes.

Lottie rushed over, hands planted on her hips, scolding Lewis.

Camden sopped the remaining dampness from his face. His coat and cravat were a lost cause, clinging to him and reeking of a brewery. "You never had any intention of helping me, did you, Sophia?"

She sucked in a small breath—whether from his question or his use of her given name, he didn't know. "I did what you asked." She took the rag from his hands and wiped under his right ear, then along the edge of his collar.

His breath caught. "But their loyalty to you is stronger than that. Have you earned it? Or are you betraying it?"

She wiped a puddle of ale on the edge of the bar before it dripped to the floor. "I don't betray the people I care about."

He took the cloth back. "I'm sending you home."

"I thought you needed me to tell everyone to cooperate."

"I think we both know that will be useless. Go home so I can beat the truth from them."

She blanched. "I won't let—"

Camden scowled. "You truly expect me to hurt Mrs. Haws? Or perhaps it's the elderly man who owns the livery stable? What kind of man do you think I am?"

"The kind that thinks me a murderer."

"Lady Harding!"

Camden turned toward the voice behind them. Sophia's gardener hovered in the doorway of the tavern, hat twisting in his hand, wrinkled face flushed. "I'm sorry to interrupt, my lady, but you are needed back at the house."

"Did you find the shooter?" Camden asked.

Wicken rubbed his disheveled tufts of hair. "No, nothing like that. Just a household matter."

Ah, this was a rescue then. "Go back to your house, Sophia."

Sophia's lips thinned.

"Unless you wish to tell me the truth."

"I do not know it."

With poise befitting a queen, she glided to the door, only pausing when Wicken stopped to ruffle Lewis's blond hair.

"Grandda." The lad glowered up from where he was scrubbing the floor, but fondness underpinned the scowl.

This whole investigation was taking far too much time. That fool Ipswith might have already devised an algebraic solution. The man would be unbearable if he succeeded first. And he'd use the clout to make sure the Mathematical Society studied worthless things each more esoteric than the next, continuing to keep their backs turned from people who had more practical needs.

Camden wiped a remaining drip of ale from his temple. He wasn't an investigator.

But he knew someone who was.

Chapter Six

Camden sagged exhausted in the rickety chair. Across from him, Gabriel Huntford, Bow Street Runner, ate some bread and cheese, his attention never leaving the door.

"You could have waited for me to come home. You didn't need to track me down in the streets of London."

But he had. Time was wasting. He needed to convince Huntford to investigate before he lost too much time from his studies.

And before his uncertainty about Sophia drove him mad.

He briefly recounted the facts thus far.

"You took your suspect to interview witnesses?" Huntford asked, a brief grin flashing over the weary lines of his face. The momentary humor lifted years of harsh living from his face, making him resemble the young man Camden had known at Oxford.

Camden sighed and picked up his tankard, grimacing at both his stupidity and the vileness of the ale.

"Trust me. This is one of the better taverns on the west side," Huntford said.

The barmaid sauntered back to the table, a plate of mutton in her hand. "Compliments of the house, constable."

Huntford shook his head. "I don't think—"

The coy look disappeared from the maid's face. "Please, Mr. Huntford. It's the least I can do. If it weren't for what you did for my Melvin—"

Huntford cut her off with a coin pressed into her hand. "I'll take your fine food. But I insist on paying for it. Your little ones need to eat, too."

The maid blinked through red eyes as her hand closed around the money.

Huntford shifted uncomfortably as the woman walked away. "Shall we walk and talk at the same time? I have work I must do." He wrapped up the mutton in a handkerchief.

The London air crowded Camden's lungs, heavy with smoke and soot as they left the inn. He turned up his collar and Huntford followed suit.

"I suppose this would have been easier if I'd waited till morning." But once the idea had occurred to him, he'd acted. When he decided something needed to be done, he was incapable of not doing it.

"Or you could have written," Huntford pointed out.

"Would you have left London?"

Huntford sighed. "Perhaps not, but I could have met you in a better neighborhood." He pulled the napkin from his pocket and handed it to a small girl huddled in a doorway. She sniffed it suspiciously before a grin lit her haggard face. She took a bite. Her eyes closed, and she chewed slowly, savoring the morsel of stringy meat.

Surely they could do better for the child. But Huntford

stopped him before he could retrieve any coins. "The other children will beat her for the money. It's better to leave her alone."

Camden's hands fisted. The large meals that had gone uneaten while he'd worked now seemed obscene.

"So the widow is your primary suspect?" Huntford asked, bringing Camden back to the reason he had come.

"I no longer know." Camden explained about the shooting that morning. Morning? Hell, it had been a long day.

Huntford glared at the prostitute who'd started slinking toward them. The woman shuffled off. "Could she have arranged for the shooting to make you doubt her guilt?"

Camden hadn't even considered that. He shifted through possibilities in his head. "No, I do not think so. She had no idea I was coming to visit her. I gave her no notice. And I saw how shaken she was. I don't think her reaction was feigned."

Huntford nodded. "It also wouldn't have made sense for her to stay around after the murder. Why not return to London or to her family?"

"So you'll investigate?"

"I don't leave London often."

"Weltford is only two hours from here. Think of it as a holiday."

"I see you still think you're humorous." Huntford paused briefly to peer into a dark alley, then continued on.

Camden shrugged. He no longer expected anyone else to think so.

"I might be able to come in a day or two. I have to testify in court tomorrow."

"The sooner I can hand off this bloody case, the better. I wasn't meant for this."

Huntford drew deeper into his jacket. Camden cursed his words. Huntford hadn't intended to become a Runner. He'd been forced into it by his sister's murder. "I'll come when I can," he said.

Camden wasn't free yet, then. Someone had tried to kill Sophia. He couldn't simply sit back and do nothing for several days. "I'll continue the investigation until you arrive."

He reworked his schedule in his head. If he investigated during the day, he could work on his equations in the evening. If he worked late, he wouldn't lose too much time. He knew from his years in the army that he could get by on three hours of sleep a night for several days. By the time he keeled over from exhaustion, either he would have found his suspect or Huntford would have arrived. "Any tips to save us both trouble?"

Huntford laughed, but it was a bitter sound. "Why are you so interested in this case? Investigation isn't your responsibility as justice of the peace."

Camden skirted around a dead rat. "I have an issue with unsolved problems." At least that's what it had been. Now his desire for the truth warred with his desire to find out more about Sophia.

Huntford suddenly reached out and grabbed a man walking past them by the collar. He shoved him up against a brick wall. "Jessup. I've been looking for you."

The wiry man swore, struggling wildly against Huntford. "Ye haven't got a thing on me, ye bloody, ruddy beak."

"That's interesting, because those false guineas came from your workshop."

Camden almost missed the dark shape that loomed on his

right. He reacted without thinking, his arm swinging up and blocking the cudgel angling toward the back of Huntford's head. He yanked away the piece of wood, slamming it into the ribs of the heavy-set attacker. While the man was doubled over, Camden grabbed his arm and twisted it behind his back, pressing him against the wall as well.

Huntford's head whipped over. "Fint, I should have known you'd be lurking behind Jessup." He nodded his thanks to Camden. "You might be better at this work than you give yourself credit for."

They forced the struggling men to the nearest night watchman's box, where they were tied while Huntford arranged for them to be transported to the nearest prison.

Huntford kept close to them as they awaited the prison wagon. Bleakness returned to his eyes. "If it's Lady Harding that interests you"—he held up his hand when Camden would have protested—"I should warn you that most of the time, the murderer is someone your victim knew and most likely knew well."

Like Sophia.

Hell.

Camden nodded, ignoring the churning in his gut. Simply because the girl had once written him a love letter didn't mean she wasn't capable of evil. She was obviously hiding something. And just because she inspired loyalty in those around her, that didn't mean she'd earned his. "You think it's Lady Harding?"

Huntford shrugged. "I've never met the woman. I can only tell you the patterns I see every day." He rechecked the ropes on his prisoners.

A young man ran to the night watchman's box, his face flushed and damp with sweat.

Huntford straightened. "Kent?"

The earnest, fresh-faced constable braced his hands on his knees for several seconds before he could speak. "A murder." He gulped in a breath. "Girl strangled. In a white nightgown. At St. Gertrude's."

"Kent, stay to help with these two." Huntford was halfway to the door before he looked back at Camden. "Do you need a place to stay for the night? You are welcome to sleep at my home."

But Camden could see Huntford straining toward the door as he spoke. "No, I'll return to Weltford." If he rode out immediately, he should be able to arrive home shortly before dawn, allowing him a few moments to work on his equations before collapsing. Then he could sleep until it reached the polite time for morning calls.

Then he'd press Sophia hard.

In a perfectly non-physical sense, of course.

Huntford disappeared into the darkness only to suddenly reappear in the doorway. "Keep in mind if Lady Harding isn't your killer, then she probably needs your protection. Either way I'd take this opportunity to become well acquainted."

Camden exhaled, an unaccountable excitement pouring through him. Huntford was right. She might need his protection. Before he surrendered to the comforts of home, perhaps he should pass by the Harding estate and make sure all was well.

Chapter Seven

Sophia drew back deeper into the shadows as a drunken farmer stumbled out of the tavern. If Lord Grey found her, he'd undoubtedly send her to prison without a second thought. Thankfully, he spent his evenings buried in his studies.

Good heavens, how much could a man drink? She knew Tubs had gone into the tavern at ten o'clock this morning. He had to go home eventually, didn't he?

She needed to find out what he knew. She'd seen the way Lord Grey's eyes had darted to him this morning when he was speaking of his source. The information must have come from Tubs.

If only she could approach him in the tavern, but she feared news of the conversation getting back to Lord Grey, and that was a risk she wasn't willing to take.

Hence, her present position huddling in the cold behind some withered bushes. She brushed a stray raindrop from her cheek.

What did Lord Grey think of her? After the shot this

morning, she thought he might have softened—she rejected the musings. She no longer cared what men thought of her. She pulled the shawl tighter about her shoulders, wishing she could shield herself from the memories as easily.

Sophia crept through the corridor toward her room. No one would notice if she disappeared from the ball for a few minutes. True, the ball was supposed to be in her honor, but after the obligatory dances from her father and brothers, she'd spent the last two hours wilting in her mother's shadow, bored out of her wits. No one would notice if she slipped away. They never had before.

"Confound it!" The quietly uttered oath stopped her.

Her brothers and father were back in the ballroom and that voice had been unmistakably aristocratic. Perhaps someone had gotten lost? Or was looking for a place to tryst? They had better not select her room. Eww.

The thought gave her the courage to round the corner. It was Richard, Viscount Harding. Blond, refined, and currently disgruntled. Not how she had dreamt of their first meeting. She tried to jerk back out of sight but it was too late.

"Lady Sophia?"

She desperately wished for a fan to hide the heat in her cheeks. Yet he knew her name. Don't ruin this. Please, don't ruin this, she begged herself.

"It is Lady Sophia, is it not? I've seen you watching me."

She would die of shame now.

"Do not be embarrassed. I find it flattering. I apologize for wandering your home, but I seem to have spilled some sherry on my waistcoat, and I'm sure you understand that I cannot be seen blemished."

He was perfection—with or without the stain. "I'm sure everyone will be too fascinated by you to notice." Foolish. Foolish. Why did she have to betray her feelings to men who had no interest in them? Was she truly so pathetic? Yet she should try to see if she could lend aid. That was the one thing she did well. "Let me fetch a servant to see to your clothes."

But Harding smiled and offered her his arm. "If my waistcoat proves salvageable, would you care to take a turn with me on the terrace?"

Shouldn't he ask her to dance? But a thrill traced down her spine. This was it. Her chance to join his glittering crowd. She relished the thought of being seen on his arm and the looks of disbelief—perhaps even envy—that would be cast her way.

"Come, surely you're not afraid to be alone with me." Then he grinned. A wide, seductive grin meant only for her. "I wish to know more of you."

The shawl around her shoulders was wool, not silk. Sophia escaped the memories by forcing her attention back to the sharp pinpricks in her toes, warning of impending numbness.

She'd been a fool. She'd feared being forever passed by and forgotten, so she'd leapt at a man who'd sought her out. Who always wanted her at his side, even if it was so she could shower him praise before his friends. It hadn't occurred to her until far too late that that kind of relationship might eventually not be enough for either of them. Soon her words weren't enough to sate his vanity, and in his opinion, that was her flaw—not his. She'd been young and in love enough to believe him for a while. She'd been nothing more than a pet so desperate to belong, it would take a kick and come crawling back. Just for the scraps of affection he'd toss her.

And that's why she'd hated Richard most of all—for showing her how weak and cowardly she truly was.

But no more. She was changing. When she found a wall inside herself, she knocked herself against it until she emerged bruised, bloody, and stronger on the other side. She wasn't there yet, but she would be.

The door to the tavern opened and Tubs stumbled out— or more accurately, Mrs. Haws shoved him out.

Sophia slipped around her bush and fell into step behind him. She hugged her arms tightly against the cold as she walked. She'd didn't fear Tubs, but what if he did have information that proved her father or brother had been involved? Would she be willing to buy his silence?

Yes.

And if he refused, she'd go to Lord Grey and confess to the murder before he had a chance to make the connection to her family.

"Mr. Spat?"

Tubs whirled around, but his motion was too quick for his inebriated state and he toppled toward the wall of tavern. He laughed as it caught his shoulder, holding him upright. "Ain't no one calls me Mr. Spat except Mrs. Spat. Hold still so I can see who I'm talking to."

Sophia hadn't moved.

Tubs blinked, craning his head from side to side. "Too scrawny to be Mrs. Spat." He leaned forward, then had to reach for the wall again as he started to tumble forward.

"It's Lady Harding."

Tubs straightened. "Is it really? Well, upon my soul. Perhaps I did have too much drink for once." He laughed, his whole body quivering.

"I had a question about what you saw in the tavern after my husband's death."

Tubs shook his head and backed up. "Ain't no way I'm talking about those two. Might come back and off me, too."

"You told Lord Grey."

Tubs listed away from the wall, loudly smacking his lips. Sophia darted to his side and braced her hands against his shoulder before he could fall. If he hit the ground, she might lose him to sleep for the night.

"I did tell Lord Grey. He gave me a guinea for it, too. Will you give me a guinea?"

"Yes." Actually she'd give his poor wife the guinea, but it amounted to the same thing.

"Oh well, then. I guess it can't hurt. As long as you don't tell them I told you."

She grunted as his weight swayed back toward her, and she pushed desperately against him. Her shawl slithered onto the cobbles, but she didn't dare risk letting go long enough to pick it back up. "I won't say a word."

"Well then, there were these two blokes—"

"You mean gentlemen?"

He tapped her soundly on the nose. "They were no more gentlemen than I'm the prince regent."

She batted away the hand still thumping on her face. "How did you know they weren't gentlemen?" She wanted to grab his fleshy cheeks and make him focus, to make him realize how vitally important his next words were.

"Their English were worse than mine. And they talked about getting paid to off the viscount. No offense meant, my lady."

She shook her head both to forgive his words and to clear the buzzing.

"And why would a gentleman off a man for a few quid? He wouldn't dirty his hands at all, most likely."

They were innocent.

She followed Tubs's example and planted her hand against the wall, gripping the cold, damp rock. Her father and brother were innocent. Her breath shuddered from her until she finally rested her cheek against the stone, sucking in the earthen, moldy smell.

Heavens, what had she done? She'd let all this time pass without doing anything to find the killer. Then she'd interfered with Lord Grey's investigation.

Did her regret mark her as a hypocrite? After all, the murderer had accomplished the same goal: freeing her from Richard.

She pressed her fist against her lips. She'd hated Richard. He had been a cruel and insecure man, but was that excuse enough to kill him? The thought had occurred to her once or twice in her darkest times. Could she have killed him herself? The gun she'd bought was to be used to scare him. To keep him from touching her again. But what if he'd tried?

She owed Lord Grey an explanation.

With a groan like a heifer giving birth, Tubs toppled to the ground.

Bother. What was she supposed to do about him? She

couldn't leave him there. It was her fault he hadn't walked straight home.

She poked him in the shoulder. "Mr. Spat?"

No response.

"Mr. Spat?" She shook him this time, although her effort didn't move him. It did, however, loosen her bonnet and send it tumbling end over end down the street in a gust of wind.

Ignoring the alarming rate at which she was losing clothing, Sophia grabbed his arm and pulled, but she could barely lift that, let alone his entire body.

She glanced down the dark street. She had two options. She could either hurry home and wake her footmen and grooms to help carry him, or she could walk to the edge of the village and find Tubs's house. Perhaps his wife and sons could help.

With either scenario, she'd have to explain why she was out unescorted in Weltford in the middle of the night.

Maybe she could leave him. After all, this couldn't have been the first time he'd failed to make it home.

A raindrop plopped into her hair and trickled down her temple. She wiped it away with a sigh.

She couldn't leave him. The man was lying with his mouth agape. He might very well drown before he awoke, although it would be a slow death; the rain was widely spaced but heavy, as if the drops had decided to band together before falling.

Standing over him while she thought, she tried to shield Tubs as much as she could. The most sensible thing to do would be to get his family's help. This way, she'd be limiting the witnesses.

Perhaps Lord Grey wasn't too wrong in thinking her a criminal. Hiding her deeds came far too easily. But then she'd perfected that for the past three years—skulking, hiding, giving partial truths.

"Lady Harding!"

She whirled around at the shouted voice, hollowed out by the wind.

Lord Grey.

Of course it was.

He sat astride a monstrous black horse, his greatcoat billowing in the wind. His hat was pulled low against the wind, obscuring his face.

"I would ask what you are doing, but I'm tired of lies." The thin veneer of politeness that had smoothed their interaction earlier had been stripped away.

"I—" She opened her mouth to explain but then realized she had absolutely no idea how to start. With the apology or with the witness lying motionless at her feet?

"Is he dead?"

That snapped her out of her confusion. "No, he most certainly is not!" She glanced down at Tubs's chest to make sure. It lifted and fell in slow intervals.

"What are you doing here?"

The apology apparently would wait. She'd start with an explanation. "I was talking to him when he collapsed from too much drink."

Lord Grey swung down off his horse and stalked toward them. He paused directly in front of her, his gaze sweeping her damp hair and clinging black dress.

She suddenly wished he could see her to advantage just

once. Out of her mourning blacks, which she knew suited her not all, and in pretty colors with her hair coiffed and styled. But no, Richard had been all about using looks and clothes to his benefit. The new Sophia no longer cared about being thought pretty and stylish.

Except a small part of her still did.

The same part of her that had desperately wanted Lord Grey to notice when she was fifteen.

He bent over and inspected the man lying on the ground, then strode toward the tavern. He returned a moment later, swinging a wooden bucket.

With a quick heave, he flung the water onto Tubs's face.

Tubs sat up with a sputter and outraged gargle. "Whatever were—what am I doing here?"

Lord Grey offered him a hand and helped him to his feet. "Go home, Tubs."

The man blinked at the two of them. "Why'd you have to ask me what I saw? Couldn't you just have asked him if he were standing here?"

"Go home, Tubs," Lord Grey repeated, his face blank, and Sophia wanted to beg Tubs to stay. But she didn't. She wouldn't beg. Never again.

Tubs shuffled off, holding his hand over his head as if that would block the rain.

Then Lord Grey advanced.

CHAPTER EIGHT

Rage blurred the edges of Camden's vision, mixing with the rain to obscure everything but the woman in front of him. He'd spent the entire bone-aching ride convincing himself she was innocent. Reinterpreting every detail until it exonerated her.

Now he'd found her in a dark village street, standing over the inert form of his only witness.

His breath escaped in harsh, shallow breaths. His anger had nothing to do with the fact that she was out unprotected in the middle of the night. Or that she'd somehow lost her bonnet and wet rivulets of hair clung to her face, making her appear more waif-like and fragile than ever. She didn't even have a blasted shawl.

Except Camden couldn't to himself.

It had everything to do with that. Which only angered him further. Why did the first woman to catch his attention in months have to be a murder suspect? "Do you at least have a coach?"

She shook her head, her chin lifting to a stubborn angle,

or at least it would have appeared so if she didn't look like a drowned kitten. "I walked here. I can walk home." She spun and began striding determinedly down the street.

Like hell she would.

He caught her shoulder.

Sophia screamed, striking out wildly against his hand. Her other fist would have connected with his nose if he hadn't jerked out of the way.

He caught her arms and held them to her sides. "What the devil, woman—"

But her eyes weren't focused on him. They were blank, terrified.

He tried to hold her as gently as he could, but her thrashing made it difficult. "Lady Harding." Was she mad, then? Is that why she didn't seem a murderer? Was she lucid one moment and insane the next? Was this why the villagers were so quick to protect her? "Sophia!" Her eyes suddenly connected to his. Her face drained of color. Her wild struggle ceased. Camden loosened his hold and stepped back.

She whirled around and ran.

Camden started after her, but a hand clamped on his arm.

"I heard the scream from the tavern," Mrs. Haws said, wincing as Sophia slipped and stumbled on the cobbles as she fled. "Leave her be."

Someone had shot at her that morning. Mad or not, he couldn't let her find her way home unescorted in the middle of the night.

But Mrs. Haws wouldn't let go of his arm. "I'll send Mr. Haws to watch after her." She exhaled heavily. "If you want to know what she's hiding, come with me."

Camden hesitated for a moment, then turned away from Sophia's retreating figure, never more aware of the damp that had seeped through his coat or the weariness in his bones. He fetched his horse and settled him in the stable before going to the tavern.

Mr. Haws, grumbling about his lonely bed, left as Camden entered. Mrs. Haws motioned to a table by the fireplace. Before Camden had removed his hat, coat, and gloves, she'd returned with a steaming bowl of beef stew, a loaf of bread, and a slice of currant pudding. She arranged them on the heavy oak table in front of his chair.

Sitting, he raised an eyebrow. "This is a little different than having ale thrown in my face."

Mrs. Haws's round cheeks darkened. "Well, we appreciate all you do for Weltford, Lord Grey. Surely we do. But we have a special place in our hearts for Lady Harding."

Camden braced himself for the explanation that was about to come next. If Sophia was mad, could he send her to trial, where she'd surely hang? As hungry as he was, he couldn't bring himself to touch the food. "You said you had something I needed to know about Lady Harding?"

Mrs. Haws twisted her hands in her apron. "Now I don't tell you this to gossip. I'm not that kind of woman." She paused, contemplating her next words until Lord Grey thought he'd go mad himself.

"Lord Harding was the cruelest son-of-a-horse-bastard that ever disgraced this town. If it wouldn't be unchristian, I'd spit on his grave."

Camden had no idea what to make of that. It was as if he'd added two plus two and gotten an apple. "I know Lord Harding was unfaithful." He'd met Harding several times around the village; he'd been pleasant, charming. Camden hadn't thought there was much substance to him, but neither had he sensed any malice.

Mrs. Haws collapsed in the chair across from him, kneading her hands together like dough. "The poor chick."

"He hurt her." He'd meant for the words to be a question, but he knew the truth even as he spoke them. When he'd grabbed Sophia's shoulder on the street—Camden cut his gaze to the fire. Now he knew why he'd recognized the blank stare on her face. He'd seen soldiers driven deep into their minds by fear. Some never to return. What had her husband done that she knew that place?

He braced his arms on the table. Had she really thought he'd hurt her, too?

"Many times. He might have had an angel's face, but his soul belonged to the devil himself."

Camden's hands clenched into fists. He should have broken Harding's dainty nose. In fact, he should have crushed him, could have. Harding hadn't been a large man. But Sophia was even smaller.

Would it have been wrong of her to kill him to end that cruelty?

The thought staggered him. He hadn't even considered the fact that the killing might have been justified.

Was that why her family had swooped in and kept things quiet? Why everyone in the town seemed happy to lie?

A log popped. The sparks that escaped up the flue were as scattered as his thoughts.

Camden wasn't one to tarry over decisions, cluttering

things with emotions. If she was guilty, then she was guilty; if she was innocent, then she was innocent.

"You know for a fact that he hurt her?" Camden asked.

Mrs. Haws nodded. "I saw the bruises myself. Wrapped a broken rib once, too." She shook her head. "The Hardings weren't here in Weltford a lot, but when they were, it was because he'd marked her up so badly that he didn't dare let the *ton* or her family see."

Camden stood, escaping to the darkness by the window, thankful for the near silence in the empty tavern to organize his thoughts. His fists ached at his sides.

He'd served in war. He'd seen countless men hewn down. He knew that some deaths were unavoidable, and some even justifiable.

Was it possible for her to have served out her sentence in advance?

Yet the law would expect him to step in if he found her guilty.

He rested his hand against the sash. Rain spattered against the glass in icy *plinks*.

Perhaps he needed sleep after all. Surely with a few hours' rest, he could make sense of all this. His prized reason and powers of discernment would return. He retrieved his coat and hat from the table. "Thank you for the information and hospitality."

Mrs. Haws rose to her feet, tugging on her apron. "Just see as you don't go judging her too harshly before you know all the facts."

Camden nodded, pulling on his hat. "I hope I never do anything without all the facts."

He had to coax his poor Archimedes out into the rain with a few carrots. He patted the horse's neck as they slipped under the punishing clouds again.

By the time they'd reached the edge of the town, the Berkshire sky had torn open completely. Archimedes's hooves sucked wetly in the mud with each step. The wind whipped Camden's coat about, allowing the rain free access to his breeches.

He soothed his horse, repeating simple equations to calm the animal and keep himself awake. Camden was so intent on explaining the simple beauty of the quadratic equation that he almost missed the sodden man passing by on the side of the road.

"Haws! I thought you were following Lady Harding."

Haws glowered from beneath a floppy farmer's hat. Water slid off the wide brim in a steady stream. "I did."

Sophia's house lay in the opposite direction.

"She changed direction about halfway and went to your house instead."

If Archimedes hadn't shifted under him, Camden feared he might have continued staring with a befuddled look on his face for an embarrassing amount of time. Why the devil had she decided to see him? Unless she planned to confess? "Is she still there?"

Haws grunted, turning up the edge of his hat so his glare would reach Camden uninterrupted. "She made it to your house. As concerned as I am about her, I wasn't about to wait around to see if she left."

Camden squinted through the rain to where the lights of his house flickered in the distance.

Perhaps she'd gone to his house because it was closer than hers.

Except it wasn't.

Camden gritted his teeth and urged the horse forward.

After several more miserable minutes, he reached the front steps of his home and was grateful to hand off his reins to a sleepy-eyed groom.

His butler opened the door. He must have been roused from his bed by Sophia, but somehow managed to appear as impeccable as ever. Perhaps the man slept like that—stiff and unmoving, his clothes not daring to wrinkle. But Camden kept his thoughts to himself. Rafferty understood his humor even less than most.

"I have taken the liberty of placing Lady Harding in the study. I have sent one of the grooms to Harding House for replacement clothing."

Blood that had been icy a moment before melted in a flash of heat. Then what the devil was she wearing—or more importantly, *not* wearing—now?

CHAPTER NINE

Sophia wrapped the blanket more securely around her shoulders, staring down at the muddy, ruined slippers she'd removed and set next to the fireplace. She'd run from him. She couldn't believe she'd run from Lord Grey like a frightened child.

But it had all happened before she even understood what her body was doing. She wasn't thinking. All she could see was Richard's mottled face.

She was supposed to be over this. She'd had three months. She'd been determined to let her fear go. Why wouldn't it obey her? It was her emotion. It should be hers to control.

Yet she couldn't. Not entirely. She still woke up in the middle of the night screaming, fighting off hands that could no longer hurt her. One day last week, she'd broken down sobbing in the middle of breakfast. And even though she knew it wasn't grief, she had no idea what it had been.

Now she was at Lord Grey's house at two o'clock in the morning. All so she could prove to herself, and to him, that she wasn't mad or a coward.

Hearing footsteps in the hall, she stood. She'd explain herself, then leave. Whatever he thought of her after that was up to him. She wouldn't go down that path again with anyone. She'd had enough of that with Richard.

Sophia's smile faded as her husband brushed past her as they entered their rooms. "Did you not enjoy the musicale? You were splendid in the yellow waistcoat."

Richard's sharp bark of laughter surprised her. "Enjoy myself? How could I when you made an utter fool of me?" The handsome man who'd wooed her was gone, obliterated by the hideous rage she'd seen flashes of over the past month. It twisted his face and aged him by a dozen years. Since then, even when he was charming, she couldn't help but see it just under the surface.

But now he'd directed it at her. Sophia swallowed, trying to think of what she could have done. In their six months of marriage, he had never spoken to her thus. She had done everything she could to make herself worthy of him. "I don't think—"

"You spent the entire evening chatting with those awful, dowdy women in the corner. Is it a wonder that Lord Charles ignored me?"

Sophia flushed. She had spent most of the evening with Catherine and Melanie. Not that she'd call either of them dowdy. They were her friends. They had spent most events together since their come-outs. Then again, she supposed they weren't the most fashionable ladies of the ton.

She hadn't intended to embarrass him.

He suddenly pulled her into his arms. "You're my wife. You belong at my side, not cowering in a corner." She blinked back a tear as he kissed her neck. "Do you think your father would be where he is today if your mother hid herself away?"

She'd be better next time. "Perhaps I can speak to Catherine and Melanie at the park or somewhere private?" she asked.

Richard nodded, his eyes pitying. "Perhaps. I don't mean to be harsh. I want you to be a credit to me."

The door opened, scattering the memory. The cheerful light cast by the candles should have softened him, but Lord Grey somehow managed to look more shadowed and imposing than he had in the street. Rain clung to strands of his hair, glittering and cold. "Why are you in my house?"

"I have been interfering with your investigation." As soon as she spoke the words, a weight dislodged from her chest.

Lord Grey ran his hands partway through his dark strands of hair, leaving them clamped on either side of his head. "I must warn you to think carefully about what you are going to say. My position as justice of the peace may force me to act."

He'd been chomping at the bit earlier in the day. Why the hesitation now? She met his eye and he glanced quickly away. She knew that reaction.

He knew about Richard. That was the only possible reason. Mrs. Haws must have told him. How much did he know?

She felt her cheeks heat with shame and wanted to pull the blanket up until it covered her head. Confound it all, Richard had been the evil one. Why must she be the one to carry his guilt? And why was so much of her loathing directed at herself?

Her hands tightened on the blanket. She didn't like that he was looking at her differently than he had an hour before. She didn't like the pity or the caution, as if she might break. She might not be strong yet, but she definitely was no longer fragile.

She hated that he couldn't see the strength that she'd worked so hard to build. For each step forward, she got yanked back three.

She intended to make up those lost steps no matter what. "I didn't kill him." She took a deep breath, loosening the grip she had on the blanket so blood could return to her fingers. "My husband. I wasn't the one who hired those two men."

"Then why interfere?" he asked, prowling closer. A wet lock of hair flopped down across his forehead and her fingers itched to brush it away.

She could feel his gaze straight through the blanket to her wet, clinging gown beneath. Where would his eyes land if she wasn't wearing the blanket? On her hips? On her breasts? Nowhere at all? "I thought I knew who was behind the murder."

"Who?" He stopped inches from her, so close she had to crane her neck to see his face clearly.

She wasn't about to plant any ideas he didn't already have. "It wasn't who I thought. That's why I'm telling you of my actions now."

"You have no proof of your innocence other than your word."

"That is correct. But I also give my word I will no longer be interfering. And I'll instruct the others to cooperate. In truth this time."

He studied her until she was sure he'd had time to count every freckle on her nose—

Her rice powder! It would have washed off in the rain. He really could see every freckle—well, let him suffer then. In fact, she resolved to never hide them again. Perhaps she'd even go out in the sun without her bonnet and get a dozen more!

Take that, Richard.

Lord Grey rested a finger against his chin. "I cannot decide if you're devious enough to claim that to hide further interference."

She supposed she deserved that, yet it still stung. "You can search all you like for proof of my guilt. It doesn't exist."

"Doesn't it?" He stretched his hands toward the fire. She found herself unable to look away from the splotches of faded ink along his first finger. The slight rosy color along his knuckles from the cold.

She felt an unfamiliar desire for him to touch her. She could imagine those hands skimming along her neck and down to her breasts. Always pleasure. Never any fear of pain. "No." She wasn't sure whether her answer was in response to his question or to her own thoughts.

He brushed the back of his finger against her cheek in a caress so light, so fleeting that she wasn't entirely sure if he *had* touched her or if she'd imagined it. "I hope for your sake that it does not."

His hand hovered an inch from her cheek. If she shifted she could press her cheek against it. She cleared her throat. "It's getting late. You should be going."

The corner of his mouth lifted. "You're the one in *my* house."

That surprised an exhale of laughter from her.

"You think I'm humorous?"

She paused, disconcerted. "I suppose I should be the one to go."

"That would simplify things." But then he stilled. "I'll take you."

She shook her head. "I will accept the loan of your coach. But I won't impose on you more than that."

His hands gently cupped her shoulders. "You were shot at this morning. Have you forgotten?"

No. Lord Grey's body on top of hers—protecting her—was proving a rather difficult thing to forget. "I sincerely doubt anyone wants to kill me enough to be waiting out in this." She glanced toward the ribbons of rain snaking down the windows.

"I'm not willing to risk that."

His words cut a slice in her heart. Once, when she was a child, her nurse had lanced a blister on her hand and it had felt like this—stinging, terrifying, and yet cathartic.

"Lady Harding's groom has arrived." The butler spoke from the doorway.

She'd forgotten the open door. Not that she'd been about do anything that she couldn't have done with an open door. "I'll be on my way then."

The butler cleared his throat. "No, my lady. Just your groom has arrived. Your coach became mired in the mud. When they tried to free it, it broke an axle."

"Is everyone unharmed?" she asked.

"Indeed. The coachman walked the horses back to Harding House while the groom came the remaining distance on foot to inform us."

"And he suffered no ill effects from the storm?"

The lines on the butler's face softened slightly. "The housekeeper has him well in hand, my lady."

"The roads are impassable?" Lord Grey asked.

Only then did it occur to her the further implication of the butler's report.

"I am afraid so, sir. I have had the blue room prepared."

Lord Grey nodded as the butler bowed and backed from the room.

"I can make it home on foot. After all, the groom made it here."

"The groom whose survival you just inquired about?"

It was hard to maintain her fierce glare.

"Besides, I'm exhausted, and in all ungentlemanly honesty, I was dreading having to escort you out into the storm."

How could she argue with that? Besides, she was a widow. She didn't have a reputation for other people to worry about. "Perhaps the butler can show me to my room?"

Lord Grey shrugged. "I can show you. It's only a few doors down from mine."

The words hung there in the air. Heavy, near-tangible things.

"Thank you," she finally managed to say, pretending that five seconds hadn't just elapsed since he'd spoken.

There was another moment of awkwardness when Lord Grey offered her his arm, only to belatedly remember she was still clutching a blanket around her.

He grimaced. "As you can see, I'm not precisely known for my social graces, Lady Harding."

She found it refreshing. Richard had known every single

blasted rule. And punished her for every lapse. She was glad there were others who had to stumble about a bit like her. "At this point, Lord Grey, I think you might as well call me Sophia."

He placed a hand under her elbow as she picked her way up the stairs, careful not to trip over the blanket. "And you may use call me Camden, if you so desire." He led her down a corridor, stopping at the door at the end of it. He gestured to the other seven doors. "As you can see, Rafferty did try to put you as far away from me as possible—unless you would have preferred the nursery upstairs. But I hear the servants have been having trouble with bats."

"I appreciate your hospitality." She tried to guess which room was his. Most likely the first one they'd passed. The carpet was a bit more worn. "Good night, Camden."

For a moment, he didn't move. His dark gaze lowered, caressing her lips as she longed for his mouth to do. Her lungs ceased to inhale, yet her body didn't care. All that mattered was whether that narrow, sculpted mouth dropped to hers.

While ridding herself of Richard's taint, she'd given a little thought to the type of widow she wanted to be. Pious and charitable? Dashing and extravagant?

Now she added another option to the list: wanton.

But Camden stepped back, allowing air to once again reach her brain.

She grabbed the door handle and hurried inside, shutting the door behind her.

After a pause, she heard Camden's footsteps as he strode down the corridor. Before she could think better of it, she opened the door a crack and peered out.

His room *was* the first one at the top of the stairs.

CHAPTER TEN

The bed was soft. The sheets were clean and smelled of lavender. She was so tired her brain felt numb.

Yet she could not sleep.

Sophia paced to the window and watched the puddles in the garden fill, then empty, depending on the speed of the rain.

Richard's hand cracked across her cheek. Black dots swam across her vision as she fell to the floor.

She scooted away, ignoring the broken mirror shards that sliced into her hands. She wanted to sob, to scream. But she had become too numb to all of this and her tears hardly ever spilled down her cheeks anymore.

This time he didn't stop with a slap. His boot hit her hip.

"Why—what—?" She tried to search his face for signs of drunkenness, as if that could explain this all away. But she knew she wouldn't find an explanation.

"You can't hold a conversation now, either."

"You cannot hit me."

"Why? Is your father going to come? Your brother? They want

nothing to do with you, apparently. We haven't received a single invitation from them in weeks."

They had, actually, but she had burned them all. She had pushed her family away—too ashamed of what she had become, too afraid to let Richard near any of them. Too afraid of what she would say to them that would make her even weaker. Now there was no one to protect her.

"You are my wife. I own you. God, king, and country say I can do what I will with you."

She tried to block as his foot kicked toward her ribs. She screamed as the blow hit her arm. She curled over, unable to stop herself from retching. The door. She had to get to it.

He grabbed a fistful of her hair. "The Earl of Statton refused my invitation to the club today. You know why? If you'd conversed with him like I told you—"

"I tried." The words whimpered from her throat. She tried even through the earl had been angered because Richard had broken his promise about supporting his bill in the House of Lords. Surely he'd seen her try, but she knew he would already have reworked the situation in his head, twisting the facts until they were what he wanted to see. "Please." She'd been careful for so long. It had been months since he'd laid a hand on her. She'd smiled and talked until her cheeks ached, wore only what he chose for her, only spoke if it was to praise him.

But she could only talk to people for so long until she could no longer hide the emptiness inside.

"Tried and failed." He flung her away. She clattered back against her dressing table, sending a bottle of perfume crashing to the floor. The smell of jasmine choked the air from the room.

"I thought I was getting a wife who would be a boon at my side. An equal." He slammed his fist into the wall by her head. He blinked slowly, then knelt at her side, gently wiping the blood from her mouth with a handkerchief, cradling her cut hand in his reddened one. "You can be, you know. Will you try?" His voice cracked and tears brimmed in his eyes. "I don't want to be this beast you've turned me into. Help me."

Sophia jerked away from the window, shuddering. If only she'd been brave enough to flee after that—

No. She wouldn't go down that path again. She couldn't change her choices. She'd made her decisions. Hating herself only robbed her of every ounce of strength she'd reclaimed.

She opened the window, sucking in air so cold it felt brittle and inhaling the smell of wet cornfields and shorn grass. With a shaking finger, she caught a drop of rain that hung heavy on the sill and flicked it to the garden below.

The rain had nearly stopped. The ripples in the puddles were now little more than tiny quivers. Perhaps she should walk home.

Her shoes.

She'd left them in the study. Sophia drew in a deep breath of the icy air. She couldn't walk home alone tonight. She wasn't a complete ninny.

But neither could she stay in this room alone with her thoughts any longer. Perhaps she could retrieve her shoes rather than waiting for a maid to find them. Then at least she could put them in front of the fire in her room so they'd be dry enough for her to brush off the mud in the morning.

She crept from her room. When she reached Camden's bedroom, she paused and listened. She didn't hear anything within.

Keeping her footfalls light, she hurried down the stairs. When she reached the study, she yanked the knob and darted in.

Into a room still lit bright with candles.

With Camden sitting at his huge mahogany desk, papers strewn all about him.

He yanked off his spectacles and shoved them in the drawer of his desk. "If you're planning to rob me, the silver's in the butler's pantry." He'd removed his coat and cravat. The top button of his shirt was undone.

She pointed rather lamely to the brown, misshapen lumps that had once been her shoes. "I thought I should try to save those."

"You could have called for a servant."

"I didn't want to disrupt your household further. I thought you'd gone to sleep." She tried not to sound accusatory. After all, it *was* his house. But he did look bone weary, dark smudges lingering under his eyes.

"I have work to do." Camden pointed to a tray perched on the edge of his desk. "Tea?"

She shook her head and took a step backward, but her foot crunched on something. She looked down to see a crumpled paper. She picked it up before thinking better of it.

"That one is worthless," Camden said, but he didn't try to stop her from opening it.

She could see bits of equations, numbers and letters, and partial graphs. "What are you working on?"

"I am trying to figure out how the roots of these blasted

polynomial equations relate to each other. If it's possible to form a general equation to find them." He said it quickly, as if he didn't expect her to either listen or understand.

She strove to make sense of his scribbles. "Why?"

He traced a disjointed collection of dots on the page. "That is the question I ask myself daily. There's a general formula for solving quadratic equations, but no one has yet found one for the quintic."

She picked up a page. "Didn't Ruffini show a general formula was impossible?"

He gaped at her, his hand hovering over the page. "He came close, but his work contains a large gap. How did you know his work?"

"I did more when I was eavesdropping on your lessons than stare at your lips."

Which of course was a terribly forward thing to say.

"Did you stare at anything else?" His leer was so exaggerated that she couldn't help the small gust of laughter that escaped her.

"I made you laugh." He tipped his head, as if studying her. No, it was more than that—it was like he was savoring her. "I like it when you laugh."

Her mirth stuck in a throat that was suddenly too dry. What did she say to that? Tell him how much she liked it, too? "Do you want help?"

"With what?"

She gestured to the pages spread on his desk.

He opened the drawer and pulled out his spectacles. "You wish to help me with my studies?"

She ducked her head, feeling a fool. "Never mind."

"Oh." He cleared his throat and put his spectacles back on. "Of course not," he concluded, his hand rubbing the back of his neck with a slow, weary motion.

He couldn't possibly be disappointed.

"Unless you needed me—"

"It's fine. I understand this isn't how normal people choose to spend their nights."

He *was* disappointed. "I would like to help if I wouldn't be a hindrance."

Some of the exhaustion dropped from his face. "You're not just humoring me?"

"No." Her father was very forward-thinking, insisting his daughters be well educated in languages, science, and mathematics. And when she'd been infatuated with Camden, she'd begun to learn on her own, reading books and treatises so that if she ever happened to meet him in the corridor she could astound him with her knowledge. But even after he'd failed to respond to her letter, she'd kept reading. She liked the simplicity of the numbers. The sheer precision of it all.

He studied her again, eyebrows lowered as if waiting for her to expose her jest.

So she added, "And how can I pass up the opportunity to stare at your lips again?"

He yanked his spectacles off. "I find myself a trifle surprised."

"At the staring or the offer of assistance?"

Those glorious lips curved. "Both. I find when I mention mathematics, it causes a mass departure from my presence. Or perhaps that is caused by my charming personality."

Sophia had no desire for charm. She knew what evils it

could hide. She preferred bluntness and honesty and a man who was comfortable spending the night in his study. "What do you need me to do?"

He leaned forward in the chair, his eyes searing her. His voice was low and husky. "I need—" He dragged his hand over his face. "You're in your night clothes."

She tugged the dressing gown tighter. It was simple wool. It must belong to the housekeeper or one of the maids. At least it was long enough to hide her bare feet. She edged them back from the hem just to be sure. "Since my gown has been taken away to be cleaned, my other option would have been far more shocking."

Camden's hand tightened into a fist around his spectacles. He thrust a sheet of paper at her. "Read these columns of numbers. They're coordinates. And sit." He pointed to a plush leather chair across the desk from him.

Their fingers brushed as she took the paper, sending sensation swirling up her fingers into her arm. She had to swallow twice before she was able to speak. "Sixteen, ninety-four."

Camden settled his spectacles on the bridge of his nose again. He dipped his quill in ink and picked up a ruler. Leaning over his page and after meticulous measuring, he drew a small dot on his paper.

He glanced up, his dark eyes expectant. She read the next numbers. Soon they had fallen into a comfortable pattern.

After a while, she helped herself to a cup of tea and one of the cakes from the tray next to it. She started to lift the lemon pastry to her lips, only to glance up and find him watching her, his lids heavy over hungry eyes. "That is my favorite."

"Oh." She held it out to him. "I'll pick another."

And suddenly she couldn't escape the thought of him leaning across the desk and taking the tart from her fingers with his mouth. Of tasting the treat on his lips.

But he shook his head, his focus on her mouth. It wasn't until he dropped his gaze back to his paper that she was able to breathe again.

She finished reading off her list, but Camden continued with his work. She supposed she should leave, but she loved watching how his lips pursed to a firm, tight line. How he'd push his spectacles back up his nose with the back of his wrist.

Sophia allowed her spine to soften and sink against the upholstered leather. Her fingers traced along the arm of the chair absently for a few minutes until she realized the pattern her fingers followed matched the creases on his forehead.

She rested her elbow on the arm of the chair and propped her chin onto her fist. Then she tucked her feet under her. A slight smile pulled at her lips. Richard would be rolling over in his grave at her lack of manners. How she wasn't chatting and charming and ensuring the man across from her was enchanted. She could sit with him in silence and feel comfortable.

That peace wasn't something she'd ever felt before, not in the home of her diplomat father, and definitely not with Richard.

But she'd found it here.

Camden rubbed the back of his neck. A faint pink light colored the room. Dawn. He hadn't expected to get anything done. But he'd preferred it to sitting in his room with Sophia asleep only a few doors down.

Now she was asleep only a few feet away.

And he'd accomplished far more than he would have imagined. It was as if her presence inspired him and awoke parts of him long dormant and unused.

Could one have a mathematical muse? Or were the words inherently contradictory?

He was a beast for not waking her. She was curled in the stiff leather chair, her head tucked into the crook of her arm. Her neck would surely be aching when she woke.

But he liked having her there. Both her soft voice as she read and now the soft cadence of her breath.

Yet he didn't want her to regret spending the night with him.

He dropped his face into his hands until images of her wrapped around him in his bed dissipated, not trusting himself to touch her until then. When the parts deep within him ceased aching, he stood and scooped her into his arms.

She stirred, murmuring something he couldn't hear, but then her face nuzzled against his chest and she quieted.

He walked slowly to her room and laid her gently in the bed. He drew the blankets over her to ward off the early morning chill and brushed a lock of her silken blond hair from her face. This close, he could see a small bump along the bridge of her nose where it had been broken before.

He barely choked back the urge to draw her into his arms again and will away every horrible thing that had happened to her.

After he'd returned home from the war with a bullet wound to the thigh, he'd almost visited her. He'd been desperate to refresh the image of the young woman he barely remembered, but whose words meant everything. It had been easier to convince himself that she'd written him the letter on a whim. She'd still been a young woman in the midst of her first Season. He'd been sure she'd find someone better. When he'd seen a notice that she'd married a few months after he returned, he thought he'd made the right choice.

What had his uncertainty cost them both?

He stepped back, watching her sleep for one more instant before he retreated to his own room.

CHAPTER ELEVEN

Sophia stretched in the bed, groaning at the stiffness in her neck. Her arms reached up across the soft down of the pillow, her toes dug down farther under the sheets.

This wasn't her bed.

She blinked her eyes open and found herself staring up at a frothy white canopy. Camden's house. How had she gotten back to bed? He had carried her. A fleeting memory of warmth and coat buttons pressing against her cheek returned.

Her cheeks burned at the thought of being held against his chest. And she hadn't even been awake enough to enjoy it.

Although she was in the blue room, there was nothing masculine about it. Ice-blue paint covered the walls, but the furniture was all dainty white French pieces with silver accents. Did he have a female relative he'd designed it for, or had it simply come that way when he'd purchased the house?

She suspected the latter, although he had surprised her last night. Who knew the man had a sense of humor?

She wanted nothing more than to stay in bed. Late mornings were the only thing she'd picked up during her marriage that she wasn't desperate to part with. She found her day went much better if she avoided as much of the morning as she could.

But she was an unwanted guest, so she couldn't justify lying in bed any longer. Besides, considering how late they'd retired, there was a good chance Camden would still be abed.

She had enjoyed the time she'd spent with him in the study far too much last night. She didn't want to meet him in the light of day and discover the pity had returned to his eyes. Not yet, anyway. Last night had been her every girlhood fantasy come true, albeit with less kissing. Perhaps it was selfish, but she wanted to have a few hours to enjoy that memory before crashing back into the reality of her life.

She also liked to think that she'd been rather bold and daring—and perhaps a bit witty—under the cover of exhaustion and candlelight. She liked leaving Camden with that impression rather than the awkward, exhausted disaster she was this morning.

When she climbed from the bed, she saw the black dress and stays she'd been wearing laid out for her. One of the parlor maids had helped her out of it last night, but she didn't want to add to the poor girl's work this morning, so she slipped them on and fumbled with the buttons on her own.

She swept her hair up into a simple knot on the back of her head. Drat. She still didn't have shoes. She checked the room again to ensure she hadn't missed them. But she didn't see them. The maids either hadn't found them yet or they were still trying to salvage them. Well, she'd go home without them. They were ruined, anyway.

She found her way downstairs. She'd find a footman, ask to borrow a carriage, then be on her way. She'd send a polite note of thanks later.

In a house this size, she would have thought she'd be tripping over servants, but she didn't see a single one. She followed the faint scent of bacon. There had to be a footman or maid tending to the food, didn't there? Sophia saw a maid walking away with a covered tray. She almost called out but didn't want to add to the gossip by shouting down the corridor.

Why hadn't she just rung the bell pull in her room? Because the butler would have certainly informed Camden when she asked for the coach.

She could catch the girl, if she hurried. Although she'd have to pass directly in front of Camden's study. But what were the odds he'd actually be there?

She quickened her step past the open door.

"Sophia?"

She froze and turned like a guilty child toward Camden's voice. He was already at his desk, papers and a large plate of breakfast arranged in front of him.

She exhaled. Really, there was no way to escape, but she tried. "I was looking for the breakfast parlor."

His attention was still on the papers in front of him. It was unfair that he could looking so delectable and well rested while she was arrayed in yesterday's ruined dress with circles under her eyes.

"I don't have one. Well, I suppose I have a parlor somewhere, but no one eats there."

"Oh."

He rubbed the bridge of his nose, leaving a streak of ink. "I don't suppose you could pretend to sleep for a trifle longer? I had hoped to get in a few hours of work before playing host."

"No need. If I might borrow your coach, I am returning home."

She finally had his full attention. He pushed away the paper he'd been working on and looked at her. "Have the roads dried?"

"The storm cleared and the sun is shining. I imagine the roads are in much better condition."

"But are they dry?" From anyone else, the words would have seemed mocking, but she knew it was merely the way his brain functioned, carefully classifying information, clarifying any ambiguity.

So she conceded. "I am not entirely sure, no."

"Then I shall send a groom to determine the condition of the road. After all, if our coaches are stranded side by side, there will be no end to the scandal."

Like the one she'd created by spending the night at his home.

"I have requested my servants be discrete about last night," he said, reading her face.

Which was indeed kind of him. But she found herself strangely unconcerned. She was a widow. And while the gossip would fascinate Weltford for a few weeks, they'd eventually move on. Especially when there was no further gossip to fan the flames.

And she had no reason at all to wish for more gossip.

"Thank you, and thank you for your hospitality."

He shrugged and shuffled through his papers. "You're most welcome. Thank you for your assistance last night."

Her stomach rumbled. Not in a dainty way that they could both pretend to ignore, but in a loud outraged bellow. She clapped her hands over her stomach but it was too late to take the embarrassing sound back. "I'll go politely back to my room and ring for a tray."

Camden was grinning, a wide, full grin that revealed perfect white teeth and creases in his cheeks. He pointed to the plate on the desk. "This is my second one. I swear I haven't touched it. You are welcome to it."

Oh, heavens. She had already barged into his house—she couldn't steal his food, too. Although the bacon did look divine . . .

"Come now, you filched my tarts last night. Why should breakfast be any different? We weren't expecting you to be up for several more hours, so you know it will take them a good while to cook your meal. And you spent the night in my bed. The least you can do is share breakfast with me."

"In *one* of your beds. Otherwise you'd be far more exhausted this morning." She primly sat in the chair facing the desk and pulled the plate closer to her, relishing the fierce pleasure in her chest. Apparently, all her wit hadn't abandoned her this morning. She'd forgotten how much satisfaction she'd always gotten from besting her brothers. They'd often worn the same shocked expression. They thought her quiet and demure. She relished reminding them there was more to her than that.

How could she have forgotten how good it felt? Ecstatic, like she'd found a trunk of jewels packed away in a musty attic.

Which made her the musty attic, but she refused to dwell overly on it.

She ate a few bites of eggs, content with his silence.

"I find myself constantly surprised by you." He sounded a bit wary, as if he wasn't a man fond of surprises.

"I have gone from suspect to houseguest to breakfast thief in a rather short amount of time." She lifted her gaze from her plate to find his deep russet eyes serious.

"Do not forget mathematical assistant."

No, how could she forget that, when it had been one of the most pleasant nights of her life?

"I find myself vexed that I cannot tell if I truly think you are innocent or if I just wish it so."

He still suspected her then. She should have known, but his easy banter had banished those memories. "Why are you convinced I killed my husband?"

He shook his head slightly. "I'm not, entirely."

Yet she was still being considered. She could sense it in his hesitation. "Do you have any reason to suspect me, other than the fact that I was married to him?"

"That gives you motive. A strong one, from what I hear. Perhaps it even justification?"

She pushed her plate away. "I will not lie to you. There were many times I wanted him dead." She stared at the fork resting on the edge of the plate. What did she tell him? What did he already know? "He"—she inhaled, the rest of her sentence escaped on her exhale—"hurt me badly."

"How badly?"

Had he really just asked her that? But with the shock came an immense relief. Everyone else tiptoed around the issue, never discussing it, never mentioning it. Even when her brother Bennett had stayed with her after Richard's death, he never asked. Everyone smiled and told the lies they had been instructed to tell. Sometimes she almost thought she'd imagined the horror of her marriage. But she hadn't. She had the scars to prove it. Both on her skin and those under it.

Most probably assumed her abuse was an intensely personal thing. It was. But she hated when people wouldn't meet her eye. Or worse, discussed her when they thought she couldn't hear, no matter how well meaning they were intending to be.

So she answered. "For the first few years it was with words. Faults he found with me. I was never good enough." She exhaled. "And I was young and naive enough to believe him. Then over the last year, his words weren't doing enough, so he began using his fists to show me how I disappointed him. How pathetic I was." She held Camden's gaze as she spoke, his calm acceptance keeping the pieces of fractured glass in her chest from shattering completely. She didn't think he understood. No one could—perhaps that was another reason they didn't try. But neither did he offer platitudes.

"How often?"

"It depended. Sometimes months would go by. Sometimes days." That was another thing she didn't think anyone could understand. Sometimes there would be these days when Richard would be kind and charming like he'd been when they'd met. She would think perhaps he had meant it when he said he'd change. But those days had been worse than the violent days, because they gave her enough hope that he could keep leading her on.

A vein in Camden's neck throbbed, and suddenly she understood there was nothing calm about his acceptance. His hands gripped the desk so tightly his knuckles had whitened.

The muscles along his jaw corded until she could see individual strands.

Her throat was suddenly hot, swollen. Each breath scoured her lungs. "Come on then," she said, bracing her hands on the edge of the desk. "Ask. Ask the question no one else has dared to voice."

"Why did you stay? Surely your family would have taken you in and protected you."

Now that he'd voiced the question, her mind blanked. How could she explain? How could she explain how everything vital had been stripped away until she was nothing but a frightened shell? How could she explain her shame over the bruises fading on her arms from where he'd grabbed her? Or say how much she hated herself?

She'd wanted to go back to her family. Longed to go sit in her bedroom and watch out her window as her mother tended her roses. Wanted to hear her sister Claire's chattering nonsense. Needed to sit in a patch of sunlight in her room with a book in her lap.

But she wasn't that girl anymore, and she wouldn't have been able to explain how she'd let that girl be destroyed.

"I believed him until I almost couldn't remember any other life. He was my husband. I didn't want everyone to know what a failure I had been." Somewhere deep inside, she'd thought Richard a broken version of her father and brothers. That he was what he was because she'd failed him. That she should have been able to be a better wife to please him and make him well.

But now she knew that men like Richard were a whole other species entirely. She'd realized it after her brother Bennett had found her injured and swooped in full of fury and grief. How could she not have seen what a pale version of a man Richard was compared to her brother?

Compared to Camden.

She redirected the conversation back to the original topic before he had a chance to respond. "But as miserable as I was, I didn't hire those men to kill him."

His lips thinned, as if from biting back words. Finally, he said, "Tubs said the killers claimed a woman hired them." His gaze examined her, burning over her skin, probing for guilt.

But she had nothing to give him but shock. "A woman?" There was a cruel irony somewhere in this. He'd betrayed her with his mistresses and one of his women had finally been brave enough to betray him in the most elemental way possible.

But who would believe her innocence? She had nothing but her word. If she were in Camden's place, she would have suspected herself. And she feared the right jury would deem it enough evidence to convict. "Why haven't you had me thrown in prison?"

"Several things point to your innocence. Someone tried to kill you yesterday. I have to wonder if it's the same person who killed your husband. Also there's the method of the murder. Perhaps if you were defending yourself, or someone else, I could see you harming Harding. Yet I cannot picture you coldly hiring two killers. So tell me, Sophia, how do I choose which set of evidence to believe?"

"Perhaps you simply need more evidence."

Damnation, but he believed her. Huntford would probably call him a fool again for telling her the details Tubs had given him, but the look of astonishment on her face had been genuine. No alarm had tainted it. "Where do you suggest I look?"

He was grateful when she resumed eating. She'd weighed almost nothing when he'd carried her to her room last night. She chewed thoughtfully as she considered his question, and he stared at the delicate line of her jaw, the narrow grace of her throat. Hell, he couldn't imagine her surviving a single punch, let alone multiple beatings.

But then her appearance was deceiving. Her recitation of her treatment at her husband's hands had taken more courage than most men possessed. She might not know that it lurked within her, but now he did.

Rarely did he meet a person who would take his bluntness without prevarications and lies. Or great offense.

Sophia had given him honesty.

He wanted to push the limits of that honesty. What would she say if he asked if he could kiss her lips? There was something simmering between them. An awareness. A connection. And for a moment by her door last night when he'd been tempted almost beyond sense, she'd wanted it, too.

Or at least he thought she had. Hell, his friends were right—he did need to get away from his studies more.

"My husband had numerous affairs. Perhaps it was a former lover or mistress."

Again, the urge to shoot the bastard surprised him. Although the army had taught him to use violence with great efficiency, it wasn't normally his first impulse.

But he would have made an exception for Harding.

Huntford had better arrive soon to take over this investigation. Camden was growing less fond of it by the second. But he didn't have the luxury of waiting, not when her life might still be in danger. "Do you know the identities of any of them?"

She set down her fork again. "A few—"

Rafferty spoke from the doorway. "There's a cart here to pick up Lady Harding."

"We will claim her ourselves, thank ye very much." Wicken barreled past Rafferty, a determined look on his face.

"You were asked to wait outside."

Wicken snorted. "I intend to ensure her ladyship leaves this house safely. Some madman shot at her yesterday and then we get word that she's somehow become stranded at this house, in need of clothing, all without ever calling for the carriage to come here. We"—he nodded to the groom that had appeared behind him—"mean to make sure she is able to get home where she belongs."

Rafferty drew himself even straighter, a feat Camden wouldn't have believed possible. "I assure you that Lady Harding's arrival at this house was entirely voluntary and any insinuation otherwise—"

Sophia rose to her feet, stepping between the two men. "Wicken, thank you for your prompt arrival, but Rafferty is correct. I desired to speak to Lord Grey but became trapped by the storm."

Wicken frowned, searching her for any hidden injuries. When he was apparently content, he bowed to Camden. "Begging your pardon, sir. In that case, we have information for you."

Camden raised an eyebrow at the switch in topic, but nodded. "Information?"

Wicken tapped the side of his nose. "Indeed, sir." He leaned back out of the doorway. "Haws!"

The tavern owner inserted himself in the group of people blocking the door.

"Tell him, Haws," Wicken said.

Belatedly, Haws pulled the battered hat off his head. "I had no idea when I spoke to you yesterday that anything had happened."

"What had happened?" Camden asked.

"Why, that Lady Harding had been shot at. I would have told you at once. I want no harm to befall her ladyship. And I want it to be clear that I had nothing to do with it."

Camden shoved the graphs and numbers in front of him to the side. "Told me what?"

"That my rifle was stolen yesterday."

Sophia's eyes flew to Camden's. He tried to ignore the small spurt of satisfaction that it was his opinion she sought. "When?"

"Careless old mule," Wicken muttered, even though he must have had Haws beat by at least a decade.

Haws folded his arms. "I'm not careless. Most of the time it's right by my feet under the bar. But I took it out Wednesday morning to clean it like I do every week. I set it on the bench by the kitchen door while I got my supplies. When I returned, it was gone. Mayhap about nine in the morning?"

Plenty enough time to for someone to steal the weapon and sneak to Sophia's house. "Who knows when you clean the gun?"

Haws stroked his hand through the bristles on his chin. "Can't rightly say. I do it every week. Anyone around the livery stable would have seen me."

Then everyone in the town was a suspect. "Who in the town wants you dead, Sophia?" Camden lowered his voice so it reached her alone.

She shook her head slightly. "I didn't think I had enemies."

"You do have one," Wicken interrupted.

Apparently Camden's question hadn't been as quiet as he thought. "Who?"

"Eugena Ovard. That evil harpy of a housekeeper."

"Why does she hold a grudge against you?" Camden asked.

When Sophia hesitated, Wicken spoke. "Ovard was close at one point with his lordship when he were young, if you catch my meaning, sir. It were when she was a housemaid and he a lad. Grew bitter over his lordship picking a wife, not that she should have believed the promises he'd made. A man like that uses promises like cheap ale. But Ovard went out of her way to add to the master's cruelty to her ladyship, to punish her. Told him lies about her. Ordered the servants not to tend her when her ladyship was hurt." Wicken grunted. "Not that we listened."

Mrs. Ovard had been quick to cast blame on Sophia, too. Covering her own crime, perhaps? Jealousy would give her a strong motive. "I'll pay her a visit," Camden said.

Sophia stood. "I'll go with you."

Chapter Twelve

"Like hell you will," Camden said.

Wicken cleared his throat rather forcefully in the door-way. Sophia watched as the color climbed up Camden's throat. But his gaze held firm. "You'll go home, where you are safe."

"I wasn't safe there yesterday," Sophia pointed out. This wasn't an argument she wanted to have in front of everyone else, but she wasn't about to back down simply because he expected her to obey. She knew the people of this town far better than he did. Especially Mrs. Ovard. Sophia needed to be there so she would know what the nasty woman was telling Camden. She'd borne her slander during three years of mar-riage, and she wasn't going to let her ruin the first tentative friendship she'd had in years with lies.

Or worse, the truth.

"You're welcome to stay at my house until I have assured you are safe."

"I've had experience with her. I can be of assistance."

Camden tapped his fingers on the desk. Finally, he stood. "Rafferty. Have the coach brought around."

"You should be leaving on the cart with me, Lady Harding." Wicken's brows drew tight. "You shouldn't have to face that woman."

"She doesn't frighten me. Not anymore."

"She frightened all the others. Still does."

"Come, Wicken." Haws patted the man on the shoulders. "She don't need your protection. Lord Harding's as dead as they get. He won't hurt any others."

Finally Wicken's shoulders drooped. "I have your word she won't come to harm, Lord Grey? I want your word as an officer. The word of a gentleman don't count for much."

Richard would have struck a servant for such an insult. Camden instead nodded, the lines of his face serious.

Wicken, Haws, and the groom shuffled out.

The room was suddenly silent. Camden walked around the desk and moved to her side. They'd been alone ten minutes ago, yet it was different to have started off alone with a man than to be left alone with one. If she reached out, her fingers would brush his chest. She wanted to rest her cheek against it to claim the memories she'd missed last night during her sleep. Her heart hammered so loudly she inched away so he didn't hear.

"Why are you letting me come?" she asked, needing something to distract her from his crisp, male scent. From the crease between his brows she'd memorized.

After all, he hadn't renewed their acquaintance by choice. He'd had years to do that, and she'd never heard from him. He'd only sought her out because he thought her a killer. She might have changed his mind, but that didn't mean he desired her.

"Were you hoping I'd be more stubborn?" He rubbed absently at the new ink on his fingertips.

"No—expecting, I suppose. I'm not used to being listened to."

"I listen," Camden said, his fingers stilled. "Besides, I have no desire to face that woman alone." His hand grazed her cheek, but unlike last night, there was no doubt he'd touched her. She felt the warmth of his hand. The tickle against her cheek. "And I'll know you aren't getting into trouble."

His hand dropped back to his side and she wanted to lift it, to turn her lips against his palm. What would he do if she did?

Almost, she had enough courage to find out. Almost.

"I'm not a woman who gets into trouble." As much as she might wish to.

Camden lifted an eyebrow. "You have been a veritable thorn in my side."

Sophia couldn't help grinning at that.

"That wasn't entirely a compliment," he said, his eyes narrowed, but a slight smile played about his lips.

"I have never mattered enough to anyone to be a thorn." As much honesty as she'd given him in the past hour, she hadn't intended to give him that much. Besides, it sounded far too much like she wanted his comfort.

She didn't.

She spun toward the door. "Shall we go?"

It wasn't until she had walked down the front steps that she realized she still wasn't wearing shoes.

Chapter Thirteen

Mrs. Ovard had the kind of pinched, bitter timelessness that made it impossible to tell if she was forty or seventy. Her high cheekbones must have given her a striking look as a young woman, but now they carved gaunt hollows in her papery cheeks.

Camden respected Sophia's courage all the more, facing this woman. He certainly didn't ever intend to come back and visit the former housekeeper unless forced to.

"—despicable manners. Perhaps I will send you back to my sister and you can starve with all the rest of her squalling brats."

The young maid—apparently a niece as well—who had let them into the cottage trembled under the old woman's wrath. "Shall I fetch the tea—"

"Did my fool of a sister rut with a donkey to produce you? No. No tea. These people are not guests and will not be staying." She whirled on them, or rather on Sophia. "I don't know what you think you have to say to me, but I have no desire to hear it." Her lip curled as she surveyed Camden. "And you, apparently, failed to listen to my warnings."

"I heard your accusations. I just failed to find any truth in them."

"How did she convince you of her innocence?" The vulgar accusation in the woman's tone made her suspicions clear.

Camden moved closer to Sophia, trying to shield her from some of the woman's cruelty.

But Sophia spoke, her voice calm, her back straight. "The evidence did that."

"Are you sure you didn't beg?" Her sneer spread wrinkles over the entire left side of her face. "You were good at that, I remember. I've always wondered if that's how you convinced Richard to marry you—or if you just spread your legs."

Sophia stiffened but did not reply.

Mrs. Ovard crowded her. "I want you out of my house, you worthless thief."

Thief? That wasn't the epithet Camden had expected. Mrs. Ovard must have seen his interest because she planted her hands on her waist. "Lord Harding had a large amount set aside for me in his will. But did I ever see a penny of it?"

"There was no money," Sophia said, resignedly. "He didn't leave any money for anyone despite whatever promises he made. As I'm sure you know. His solicitor finished settling the estate last week. I know you met with him."

"The pension you gave me isn't enough for a dog."

Sophia had provided her with a pension? The woman should have been turned out into the gutter. In fact, he almost hoped Mrs. Ovard was guilty. He wouldn't have any qualms sending her to prison. "Where were you yesterday morning?"

Mrs. Ovard stiffened. "What business is that of yours?"

"Someone tried to shoot Lady Harding."

The color fled from Mrs. Ovard's face, leaving it a sickly yellow. "I was here. My maid will vouch to that."

Camden glanced over at the maid, who was staring at Sophia. As he watched, the young girl straightened, copying Sophia's bearing and expression.

Mrs. Ovard drew back as if she'd been slapped. "Don't go getting above yourself, Margaret, and do not dare lie. Liars burn in hell."

Margaret's courage lasted for another minute, then crumpled along with her face. "She was here. She wrote letters and had tea with the vicar's wife."

Mrs. Ovard collapsed into a nearby chair.

"You could have hired someone. Like you hired someone to kill Lord Harding," Camden said, not feeling particularly merciful.

"I wouldn't have killed Richard." For a moment she clutched her chest, grief twisting over her face. "He may have been fool enough to marry her. But at least he realized his mistake."

Margaret spoke up again from the corner. "If the killer was hired, it couldn't have been her. She spends every last pence her ladyship pays on laudanum. Stirs it in her tea. Even when the vicar's wife is here."

Mrs. Ovard leapt to her feet, lunging for Margaret, her fingers curving into claws. "I'll beat you for your insolence."

Sophia stepped into the housekeeper's path. "My husband may have been large enough to beat me, but you are not. And you will have to pass through me to get her."

Camden wasn't entirely sure. Mrs. Ovard was a good six inches taller.

But then he saw Sophia's eyes.

Mrs. Ovard had no idea the danger she was in.

Or perhaps she did, because she froze, her hands dropping to her sides.

"My husband may have been allowed to strike me, but if you so much as lay a hand on Margaret, I will press charges."

Mrs. Ovard inched backward, her knees bumping against her chair. "Oh, will you? And what will you do if I tell the court every little dirty thing I know about you and your husband?"

Sophia gave a half smile. "You and Richard really would have been perfect for each other. But I no longer care what the world thinks. And for everything you say against me, I will reveal one of your secrets. Come, Margaret. I find myself in need of a new maid."

"*What?*" Mrs. Ovard shrieked. "You worthless, gutter—"

Neither Sophia nor Margaret looked back.

But Camden did. "You seem to labor under some confusion, Mrs. Ovard. Lady Harding is no longer defenseless and without a protector. Your foul abuse of her character will cease at once or I shall take a close look at the inventory of things that went missing at the same time you were let go from Harding House. Understood?"

Her silence was the closest thing he supposed he'd get to acceptance. He followed Sophia out into the street, feeling the need to pull clean air into his lungs. She stood a few yards down next to the coach, her head bent over the young girl's. Margaret nodded, her braids bouncing before she practically skipped away.

Camden stopped at Sophia's side, speaking her name softly so he didn't startle her before placing his hand on her lower back to assist her into the coach. She still she spun toward him, though, but this time her cheeks flushed with triumph and her sapphire eyes sparkled. "I did it. I faced her." She accepted his hand and climbed into the forward-facing seat.

Unlike her normal serenity, she shifted excitedly in her seat as if the elation in her fought to free itself.

She could have no idea how alluring her courage in defense of the maid had been.

Or the fantasies her fierce defense had inspired. How he'd wanted to pick her up and carry her to the privacy of his carriage where he would follow her triumphant flush past the neckline of her gown and see how far he could make it spread.

He only wished her defense of herself had been as staunch.

She grinned, leaning forward. "You can have no idea how long I've wanted to do that." Then suddenly she stood, and before he could ask her what was amiss, she leaned forward, braced her hands on his knees, and kissed him. Her lips were quick, soft, fierce. Obliterating his paltry fantasies with the throbbing ecstasy of reality. "And that as well."

CHAPTER FOURTEEN

Up this close, she could see a thin circle of amber around the dark brown rims of his pupils, the slight indent on the bridge of his nose from his spectacles. The warmth of his breath brushed across her lips.

She tried to savor it all.

Because Camden still hadn't moved. And she was positive he'd never let her this close to him again.

She was a fool to think that he wanted her kiss, but her victory had made her feel brave. She wasn't the type men dreamt of. She was plain and pale, almost to the point of being invisible.

But then Camden touched her. Starting at the very tips, he dragged his fingers over the back of hers, then across the skin on the top of her hands. By the time his fingers reached the inside of her elbows, her arms trembled. His hands continued up her arms to her shoulders, then his thumbs swept inward along the high, proper neckline of her gown. No closer to impropriety than her collarbone, the lowest the collar allowed him. She'd never hated wearing mourning more than at that moment.

She wanted to sway forward and kiss him again. But her moment of confidence had passed, drained away by old fears. He had to be the one to kiss her. She had to know he wanted her. That he was more than pitying her. That she wasn't as lacking as Richard had always told her she was.

She knew she was supposed to be stronger than that. She'd told herself she was never going to allow Richard's poison to rule her life. But what if that part hadn't been poison? She'd never kissed another man. What if her kisses were as pathetic and unstimulating as he'd claimed? Richard had been a good kisser. At least that's what other women had sighed about, but for Sophia it had always been awkward. She'd never been sure if she was doing it correctly. If she should apply more or less pressure.

Camden's lips claimed hers, and all thoughts fled.

His mouth brushed hers—once, twice—before he wrapped his arm around her waist and pulled her into his lap. His mouth sought hers again, this time without hesitation. His tongue traced the seam of her lips, but when she parted them, he didn't plunder roughly. Instead, he continued to explore the soft flesh of her lips, awakening every nerve ending. Sensitizing the skin to the point that when he gently raked his teeth across her bottom lip, a moan rasped from her throat.

She threaded her fingers through the short strands of his dark hair, struggling not to shift wantonly in his lap and reveal the extent of the tension between her legs. But the tighter she held herself, the closer it brought her to the brink of release.

She'd spent many hours imagining kissing Camden when she was a young girl. And perhaps a few more since she'd met him again yesterday.

Her imagination needed some serious work.

Her back arched as his hand slipped down her spine. He kissed the way he solved his proofs: slow, intense, thorough. He didn't move on until every sensation had been fully explored. Until every pleasure had been magnified.

As his tongue twisted with hers, she could no longer keep her hips still. She shifted against him, pressing closer.

They both froze when her hip brushed against the evidence of his arousal. Wild passion glittered in Camden's eyes, so different from his normal methodical analysis. His chest heaved against hers.

Not once had she thought the kiss awkward. Not for a moment had she even had time to think or analyze her actions. She'd simply been swept away.

Camden's finger traced back and forth across her lower lip. "You've been wanting to try that?"

She licked the tip of his finger as it crossed the middle of her lip. "I had to know if I was capable."

Her backside hit the seat with a thump as Camden removed her from his lap. The heat in his eyes cooled. "Why did you kiss me? Because you wanted to kiss me or because you had something to prove to yourself?"

She knew she'd offended him, but she owed him the truth. "Both."

Camden crossed his arms across his chest. "I find myself less than flattered, but what was your conclusion?"

"That I should have been braver and ambushed you in the corridor of my parents' house all those years ago."

His arms unfolded. "That would have been awkward. I, no doubt, would have been terribly intrigued and yet helpless to do a thing in return. You were far too young."

"Only by six years. You noticed me?"

"Your brother once asked me why my lectures were so much better on some days than others. I'll admit my vanity pushed me to try harder when I suspected you were listening."

Heat filled her cheeks. She wanted to ask if he'd gotten the letter confessing her girlish feelings, but what did she expect him to say? He obviously hadn't cared enough to respond then. Did she truly want to know if that had changed?

"So what were you trying to prove?" Camden asked, following the line of her jaw with his thumb.

The warmth in her cheeks turned to a raging inferno. "My husband said I"—she cleared her throat—"lacked passion."

Camden swore, but then his expression softened. "I hope you no longer believe that."

"No."

His eyes darkened. "If you have anything else you'd like to prove, I hereby offer my services."

He was flirting. Some of her shock must have shown because he dragged his hand over his eyes. "I apologize if that wasn't appropriate. I realize you are still in mourning. I do better with numbers than people."

"I do not mourn him."

"No, but I doubt you are looking for someone to take his place yet."

In her bed or in her heart? Which position was he considering? Both? "I kissed *you*, if you recall."

"Did you intend for it to go beyond the single kiss?" He shrugged at her silence, as if proving his point.

It took her a moment to gain the courage she sought. "What if I did?"

Camden's rough exhale was interrupted by a tap on the window.

Sophia jumped. She hadn't realized Camden never had a chance to give the coachman the order to depart. They were still sitting outside Mrs. Ovard's house. That would give her something to gossip about.

"If you are ready, sir?"

Camden nodded, raking his hand through his hair. "Indeed. We will return Lady Harding to her house."

"Very good, sir." The coach swayed as the groom climbed back on his perch.

The coach lurched into motion and rattled along the rough street. Sophia turned her face and watched as the village passed, trying to make sense of her churning emotions. Only one thing was clear: she wanted to kiss him again. She wanted to do *more* than kiss him again.

Suddenly a horse screamed. The coach lurched, jolting along the cobbles with teeth-jarring speed.

Bracing his hands against the wall of the coach, Camden strained to look out the window. "The coachman's still on the box."

They heard shouts and warnings as the man tried to bring the vehicle back under control and the outriders followed behind.

Sophia gasped as the coach wove hard to the right, slamming her shoulder into the lacquered paneling. Camden braced his long legs on opposite sides of the coach, then wrapped his arms around her, keeping her tight against his body as the coach swayed again. Villagers outside screamed and cursed.

Sophia dug her fingers into Camden's lapels, praying everyone would clear the path. Strangely, her worry wasn't for herself. She felt uniquely safe in his arms. Even when Richard had still been charming, she'd always felt unbalanced around him. Yet in a coach hurtling toward destruction, she knew Camden would keep her protected.

The coachman's commands softened to soothing nonsense as the jolting slowed to a rough sway, then stopped completely.

Camden was out of the coach the moment it stopped. "What the devil happened?"

"Someone threw a rock at the horses, sir," the coachman said, his voice shallow and winded.

Sophia stood on shaky legs and went to the door of the coach. Camden assisted her down, his hand remaining on her waist afterward.

"Did you see who it was?" Camden asked.

The coachman shook his head, calming one of the horses whose nostrils still flared. "Didn't see a thing. We were passing by the market and tavern. Hit the horse square in the flank."

Camden's hand tightened at her waist, which seemed to surprise him because he then flinched away.

The abashed grooms had nothing useful to add. The

market had been filled with the usual villagers, but they hadn't seen anyone actually throw the rock.

Finally, Camden shook his head and helped her back into the coach. He settled across from her. "What changed in the past week? Why is someone attacking you now?"

She tried to think. "You started to investigate again. You thought I was a murderer. Perhaps someone agreed with you?"

Camden's face stilled. "Bloody hell, who?"

But she could think of very few people who cared enough about Richard to avenge him. Whenever they'd gone to an event, he'd always arranged to be in the center of everything. His looks and money guaranteed that. But very few people had come to the funeral.

"I don't know." She wished if a woman had cared about Richard that much, she would have stolen him away.

No, Sophia wouldn't have wished Richard on anyone.

"You won't be safe until we do."

CHAPTER FIFTEEN

Camden went over the orders with Sophia's butler one final time while she changed into a fresh gown and replaced her missing shoes. He'd arranged the footmen and grooms into patrols so there was always someone watching her house. He'd tried to convince her to stay with him until they'd identified her attacker, but she'd refused despite his perfectly logical arguments.

Camden circled the house one final time, checking windows and ensuring the patrols were in place. He wished they'd been able to create a useful list of suspects. But while the list of her husband's lovers Sophia had provided had been sickeningly extensive, all of the women were safely away in London—although it was possible one of them had hired someone. He'd have Huntford look into those when he arrived.

Wicken joined him as he finished his circuit of the house. "Any news, sir?"

Camden shook his head. "How long have you worked at Harding House?"

"Nearly my entire life. Except those few years I served in the army as a young man."

"Besides Mrs. Ovard, did Lord Harding have relationships with any village women?"

Wicken bent over to pull a weed from the gravel path. "Are there any he didn't ruin?" He yanked the interloper out by the roots and crushed it in his hand. "This house has never been the main residence of the Hardings. They prefer their estate in Brighton. But they'd come out here about once or twice a year, and whenever they left, there'd be some local girl crying after his carriage. Showing up on the doorstep looking for promised things that we had no way of providing."

"Could you make me a list?"

Wicken dropped the crushed weed from his hand and brushed dirt from his fingers. "I don't reckon if I'll be able to recall everyone."

Camden stepped around a large oak tree to see how close the branches came to the windows on the upper floors. A curtain twitched and Sophia's face appeared in a window above him. She was dressed in something white. Or not dressed. Heat surged through him as he thought of her clad in nothing but her shift. "Perhaps Mrs. Haws would know—"

"I'll check with her, sir, and get right back to you. I know you're busy, what with your work and watching out for her ladyship," Wicken said.

A scream echoed through the garden.

Camden bolted into the house, shoving past the butler and grooms, taking the stairs two at a time. Why hadn't he checked her room? He should have ensured her house was safe before allowing her into it.

Another scream, this time ending in a sob. He followed the sound toward an open door at the end of the corridor. It matched the window he'd seen from below.

"Get back!" Sophia's voice was panicked but firm.

As Camden reached her room, a maid stumbled from the door directly into him. He had to grab her to keep her from collapsing to the ground, but his attention was already focused inside the room and on whomever Sophia was warning away.

But he couldn't see anyone.

"Who—"

"Back away. Stay behind me," she said again. But this time he realized she was talking to him just as she must have been talking to her screaming maid moments ago.

He disregarded her command, stepping to her side.

A quick writhing on the floor halted him. A snake. It stilled again, its beady eyes watching. A black tongue darted out, tasting. It twisted again. Restless. Agitated.

"Get behind me," he ordered Sophia.

She glanced at him from the corner of her eye. "I think I said that first." The maid moaned again from the corridor. "Louise has a dislike of all things reptilian."

So Sophia's first urge had been to throw herself between the girl and the snake. Did it even occur to her that it should have been the other way around? How could he have thought her a murderer? She was too quick to protect those around her. Camden somehow knew that even if it had been her worst enemy in the room, she would have been the one to step in front.

But even if Sophia didn't realize she was worth protecting, he did. "Get a blanket from the next room. I'll throw it over the snake and—"

Wicken pushed past both of them, strode up to the snake, and snatched it up. Grabbing it behind the neck, he ignored the tail lashing around his arm. "How'd this get in here?"

The maid shrieked as Wicken approached her. "It was in a bag under the bed!"

Camden strode to the bed and retrieved a linen flour bag lying half-concealed under the bed. He spun toward the servants who had joined the commotion. "Who has been in this room?"

The butler wrung his hands. "I don't know of anyone, sir. Except Louise and the upstairs maid, of course."

"That would be me, sir." Another maid stepped forward. "But I swear that wasn't in the room when I cleaned this morning. And I didn't notice anyone around her rooms." She gnawed on her lip. "I don't know who'd be trying to kill her."

"Scare," Wicken corrected.

"What?" Camden asked.

"This here's a grass snake, not an adder. Not poisonous."

Camden frowned at the news. This made no sense. "This seems more like a schoolboy prank." Why would the attacks be decreasing in efficacy? Wouldn't the person have become more desperate? More violent?

Camden noticed the number of people in the doorway. "Aren't some of you supposed to be patrolling the grounds right now? What if this was a diversion?"

The butler stiffened and turned on the offenders, driving them back down the corridor.

Wicken held up the snake. "What do you want me to do with it, sir?"

Sophia answered. "Just take it out and let it go by the pond. There's no reason to harm it."

Of course she'd try to save the snake.

Wicken nodded and left, most of the servants following him.

Louise still leaned against the doorway, cheeks pale, decidedly unstable.

Sophia rested a hand on her arm. "Go rest for a few hours."

"But, my lady—"

"I shall be fine. Rest."

The maid nodded. Hugging her arms tightly about her waist and muttering about slimy, scaly things, she swayed from the room.

Sophia's exhale shuddered from her. But before he could offer the comfort of his arms, she was laughing. "I'm such a fool. Perhaps I'd have been better off if my brothers tormented me with snakes rather than frogs. Those I can identify with remarkable skill."

Her dark blue eyes met his and he couldn't help grinning along with her. A fine pair they made, ready to do battle with a garden snake. He'd spent most of his childhood locked in his room studying. His father hadn't allowed much time for adventuring.

She laughed until she pressed her hand against her stomach as if it hurt from too much gaiety.

In that instant, two things occurred to Camden. One: they were very much alone in Sophia's room. Two: her hand was pressing directly against the white fabric of her stays.

His amusement ceased.

Camden braced his hand against the bedpost for support. How the devil had he missed that small detail? The presence of a four-foot-long hissing creature, he supposed.

Sophia lifted a hand to wipe a tear from the corner of her eye. He knew he should be a gentleman and leave, but he couldn't stop himself from drinking in the sight of her first.

The soft mounds of her breasts cupped and uplifted by the support of her stays, quivering with her mirth. The almost impossibly tiny span of her waist.

Bloody, bloody hell. He'd waited too long to leave. There was no way he'd be able to do it now. Heat rose under his skin, tightening his loins.

With one move, he pulled her into his arms and brought his lips to hers, wanting to taste that joy. He wanted to catch each of her gasps, trap the warmth in her eyes, and forever banish the pain that lingered there.

For a moment, she stilled in his arms, but then with a moan, she molded herself against him, her lips responding to his.

He moved her until her back pressed against the bedpost, the primal need to get her into the bed overwhelming. His hand slid up her side and over the edge of her stays, the soft skin of her breasts rising to meet his hand. He could hear his own ragged gasps, but he was unable to control his body's reaction.

"You need to laugh more often," he whispered against the pulse fluttering in her neck.

"Apparently so." She shifted, her hips pressing against his, driving with a pleading moan. He cupped her cheek, his finger tracing her cheekbone and the delicate skin under her eyes. The pupils had dilated, leaving them dark with want, unfocused in their intensity.

He found himself stepping back. Not breaking the connection with her skin, but allowing himself room to breathe, to think. He wanted those eyes focused on him, not carried away by passion—or at least not until he was sure she wanted this.

"You kissed me first this time," she whispered. "You want me."

"Yes." She'd no doubt felt the proof of that quite clearly, but at the same time, a touch of unease knotted in his stomach. "Was this another experiment?"

"No." But there was a question to her word, a slight uncertainty.

He had her hot and willing in his arms and yet somehow that wasn't enough. She'd said in the coach she wanted to go beyond a kiss. Apparently, she was a woman of her word.

"You offered yourself for experimentation." She dragged a finger down the front of his jacket, stopping just short of the waistband of his trousers.

He forced himself to take another step away from her, until he had fully escaped the intoxicating warmth of her body. Her hand dropped away. "What precisely do you want to try?"

Everything. She wanted to strip him naked and press her lips to his chest. Kiss her way down his stomach until she could trail her tongue around his navel. But she couldn't bring herself to say those words. "I desire you." Couldn't he just kiss her again? Why did he have to talk and confuse things.

"But is this what you want?"

Her aching body begged for completion. "You kissed me," she reminded him again.

"I want what's best for you. I question whether it's me right now."

"Why do you have to ask that?" Everyone had an opinion about her well-being, didn't they? Or on what she was doing wrong. On what she could do better. On how they could keep her from ruining her own life.

She was tired of it.

"Can you honestly say you're ready for me carry you to that bed?" He reached for her again, only to let his hands drop away without touching her. "I want to, you know."

"I want that, too."

A muscle in his jaw twitched. "Are you certain? Absolutely?"

Already her head spun from kissing him. What if she coaxed things further? Her body wanted it; there was no doubt of that. But were her heart and mind ready?

Camden's finger traced the shell of her ear, then down her neck, dipping to the valley between her breasts.

She shivered.

"When you are sure, Sophia, then we will finish this."

A woman cleared her throat. They both spun. Louise stood in the doorway, mouth agape. "I remembered I hadn't helped her ladyship dress."

Camden backed away. She supposed he meant to slink away while she was distracted, but she wasn't about to let him give her condescending proclamations without a response. "We'll finish this in the library." She wasn't entirely sure which *this* she meant.

He nodded as he fled from the room. She had Louise rush her dressing, not even bothering with her hair. If it was mussed, it was Camden's fault, after all. She finally replaced her slippers and hurried after Camden.

A footman stopped her in the corridor. "Begging your pardon, but a constable from Bow Street has arrived. He claims he was hired by Lord Grey to investigate you."

Years of practice kept shock from showing on her face. He'd hired a Runner to investigate her. He hadn't believed in her innocence after all.

Was she always going to be the gullible fool, only believing what she wanted to believe?

She'd thought Richard could fix her, that his charm and popularity could pull her from the shyness she'd always loathed. But in the end he'd only broken her more badly than before. "Put him in the parlor. Tell him Lord Grey and I will see him shortly."

After a few angry strides, she flung open the door to the library. "I'll admit that I kissed you first. But then you kissed me, curse you. You kissed me and said those things while all the time you thought me a murderer. While you planned to send a constable to my house."

Camden backed away from the empty bookshelf he'd been studying. "I take it he's here?" He flinched at her glare. "I hired him yesterday."

"What do you expect him to find about me that I haven't already told you?"

Camden's brows lowered. "Nothing. I hired him before I believed you innocent. But now that he's here, he can discover who is behind these attacks on you."

That rather tarnished her righteous anger. "Why didn't you say something?"

"I should have warned you, but there has rather been a lot going on this morning."

She couldn't find fault with that statement. "In his mind I'm a suspect." She'd managed to convince Camden, but could she convince a stranger? It had been easy to claim she'd take the blame to protect her father, but she refused to take the blame for anyone else.

CHAPTER SIXTEEN

The man standing in Sophia's study wasn't Huntford.

The beefy, ferret-faced Runner sketched Sophia and Camden a quick bow and handed him a folded sheet of paper. "Your butler said I could find you here. From Mr. Huntford, sir."

Camden opened the paper.

> I am unable to leave London at this time. The new
> murder mirrors my sister's. Williamson is one of the few
> investigators at Bow Street I trust.
> Huntford

> P.S. Keep him away from your brandy.

Sophia offered Williamson a seat. The man had the build of a prizefighter and hesitated to sit in the dainty, upholstered chair, but he complied. The Runner already knew the basic details of the case from Huntford, and Camden filled him in on the rest, including the most recent attacks on Sophia.

Williamson jotted down a few notes on a small pad of paper. "I have a few questions for you, Lady Harding."

"She's no longer a suspect," Camden growled. Huntford might think this man was trustworthy, but he didn't want him anywhere near Sophia.

Williamson rubbed at a pockmark on his cheek. "She is as far as I'm concerned."

Sophia placed a hand on Camden's knee. "You had the same suspicions. I have nothing to hide."

Williamson grunted, his eyes shifting suspiciously. "I must ask about your relationship with your husband."

War had been hell, but it had nothing on the next half hour. Camden had thought his questions to Sophia had been blunt and overly personal. They were mere parlor talk compared to the things Williamson asked.

Camden tried several times to halt the interrogation. Her cool recitation of the broken ribs and nose, black eye, and dislocated shoulder roiled inside him until he feared he'd vomit.

Yet each time he tried to stop Williamson, Sophia would shake her head slightly and answer, her face as pale as paper yet perfectly composed.

Finally, Williamson stood, his gaze averted. "I'm sorry to put you through that." And it was clear from the deference in his tone that he meant it. She'd allayed his suspicions.

But Camden had to unlock the muscles in his jaw before he could speak. "Her gardener, Wicken, is compiling a list of women in the village who had a past with Lord Harding. I'd start there."

They sent for Wicken, but he'd gone to the village to speak to Mrs. Haws.

With a promise to report on his progress, Williamson left.

Sophia sank down onto a chair, rubbing her arms as if she were cold.

"You didn't have to tolerate all those questions," Camden said, hating that he'd been the one to bring all this on her. It was his fault all these wounds had been ripped open twice in one day.

"I cannot pretend my past didn't happen."

Camden dragged his hand through his hair. "I don't want you to."

"Then what do you want?" He could see the lines of strain around her mouth and the way her hands trembled on her sleeves.

How could he even begin to answer that? "I don't want Harding to be able to control you all over again every time you have to explain what happened."

"That's not what happens."

"Isn't it? You didn't want to answer half the questions, yet you did. Why? Why didn't you spare yourself?" Camden asked.

"I'm tired of the lies."

"Or were you scared?"

She rose to her feet and paced toward the windows. "I'm not a coward."

Hell, he thought her one of the strongest women he knew. He simply wished she'd use that strength to defend herself.

Sophia's butler bowed in the doorway. "One of your grooms delivered this, sir. He said it was urgent." He handed him a folded sheet of paper, sealed with a red wafer and the Greek symbols of the Mathematical Society.

Camden had already torn through the wax. It was from

his father. He scanned the contents and swore. Ipswith had called an impromptu meeting of the Society. Camden's father hinted that he thought his protégé would have revolutionary information to add to the knowledge of mankind.

"Is everything all right?" Sophia asked. Even now, her concern outweighed her anger. Couldn't she see how priceless that trait was? That she was?

"Ipswith claims to have solved the quandary."

"Has he presented it yet?"

"No." But he wouldn't have called a meeting if he wasn't close. Nothing made mathematicians bitterer than being forced to socialize for no reason at all.

Camden still had a chance to present his own solution first. If he found one.

"I think you should go work on it." Unfortunately, her anger hadn't disappeared completely.

"I should stay to protect you."

She crossed her arms. "My servants have it under control."

"Sophia—"

"You've made your opinion of me quite clear."

"Apparently not. I think you're brave." But he was a blundering fool when it came to her—that much was clear. And he'd never stayed where he wasn't wanted.

Camden said he thought her brave.

After he said he thought her a coward. That's what he'd meant when he said she wouldn't protect herself, wasn't it? He seemed to think there was some distinction between the two things, but she couldn't see it.

And she did protect herself. Hadn't she just sent him away?

The empty mahogany shelves towered over her as she entered the library. She closed her eyes and let herself picture what it would be like filled with books she wanted to read and mayhap a soft, overstuffed chair by the fireplace. Most of the images lacked focus, lacked the details she needed to give her the answers she sought.

But one she could picture clearly—Clayton laying her down by the fireplace and striping this ugly black gown from her body.

She'd been a foolish, foolish girl when she'd written the letter to Camden. She'd thought what she felt had been love. Even later, when she married Richard, she'd bittersweet fondness for memories of that love.

But she'd never loved Camden.

She'd been infatuated, fascinated, attracted. All of which had seemed like love. But it had been like oil on water, never deeper than the surface.

Now she'd plunged past that.

She wouldn't say it was love that now consumed her either, but even the first small pangs were more magnificent, more terrifying than anything she'd felt before. And she gloried in them, proud to discover she could still feel them, that something so wondrous could still grow inside her.

Now she didn't just want him to notice her. Now it was just as crucial that he understand her. That she sink deep until she knew his heart, his thoughts, his desires.

So why did she continue to flutter uselessly about, as uncertain of him as she was of her library?

Because she *was* certain of one thing. A terrifying, deliciously, scandalous thing.

She wanted him finish what they had started upstairs. And maybe—but she could sort with the rest of her feelings later.

Camden had said he needed her to be sure. Well, now she was.

A smile curved her lips.

But how exactly did she go about getting Camden as her lover? She'd never played the seductress before.

Well, one thing was certain; she couldn't do it with him banished to the other side of the village.

As she left the library, she met Wicken trudging up the corridor. "If you have a moment, Lady Harding?"

She nodded.

"Lord Grey asked me to compile a list of local girls who"—he tugged on the sleeve of his brown woolen jacket—"were ruined by Lord Harding. I've compared my list with Mrs. Haws's. And I hate to ask, but I wanted to check if you knew of any others."

He held out a piece of foolscap that contained about a dozen names of Richard's lovers. Sophia took the page and studied it. Curse him. Curse him. She hoped Richard had already been sentenced at Judgment for each and every one.

"Do you know of any more?" Wicken asked.

She shook her head. She hadn't known of half of those.

Wicken's shoulders sagged. "Good. I'll take this to Lord Grey."

Sophia kept the paper. "I'll take it to him." But no, if

she was going to try to seduce him, she wasn't going to hide behind an excuse. She'd go because she wanted to.

She handed the paper back. "On second thought, there is a Runner investigating in town. Take the list to him."

Wicken's eyes widened as he tucked the page in his pocket. "A Runner?"

"Lord Grey hired him."

"I'll go find him right away." Wicken gave a jerky nod, then folded the list and jammed it in his pocket.

"Would you have the coachman bring the carriage around? I have a matter to discuss with Lord Grey."

Camden arranged the papers on his desk and set out his ink. Perhaps if he altered his approach to the theorem slightly . . .

Two pages of worthless scribbles later, he glanced up at the clock. It had to have been longer than ten minutes. He'd never been bored by his work before. He watched the clock for a full minute just to be sure the hands were moving.

They were.

The problem wasn't with the clock, it was with him. Something was missing.

A beautiful woman in the chair across from him. Her feet tucked up under her. Her hair falling over her cheek. Her velvety voice reading his numbers. Her lips smiling at his inane attempts at humor.

With a sigh, he searched through his desk, pulling out a filthy, creased paper he'd buried in the bottom years ago. He hadn't looked at it since he'd returned home from the Peninsula, but neither had he been able to throw it away.

Dear Captain Grey,

    You are no doubt surprised to hear from me. In case you do not recall, I am the younger sister to Lord Darton Prestwood, whom you tutored earlier this year. But I hope you do recall who I am, for I haven't been able to stop thinking of you. I know war is an uncertain time, so I could not go another day without confessing the depth of my affection. I am in love with you, Captain Grey. I have been since you sought me out to bow over my hand even though I assumed I was hidden in the shadows. I realize you might not return my affection. If that is the case, I beg you ignore this letter and we shall both pretend its delivery unsuccessful. But whatever our fate may be, know that I hope fervently for your safe return.

    Yours forever,
    Sophia Prestwood

Could he reclaim this? Could he somehow remind her of the feelings she'd once had for him? What they'd shared in the library had been about passion. It had been sparked by the heat that had simmered between them the past few days. But physical desire wasn't enough. He wouldn't be satisfied with anything less than her heart

He shoved the letter away. No matter what he wanted, he had to wait until she was ready.

Returning to his work, he slowly built a list of roots from the lower equations, trying to figure out the difference between them and what he was unable to do, trying to lose himself in the tedium.

But numbers held no attraction now that he knew the

gleam of triumph in her eye before she'd kissed him in the coach. The weight of her body nestled in his lap, stockinged feet peeping out.

His quill snapped in his fingers and he tossed it away. Why did she overtake his mental facilities precisely when he needed them the most?

With a sigh, he sprinkled sand on the page before he smeared the numbers. Perhaps that was the crux of his crisis. This strange fascination was all his.

And he wasn't sure he could free himself from it.

In fact, he didn't want to free himself from it.

He put the stopper in his bottle of ink. Hell, he couldn't focus anyway. He might as well go ensure Sophia was safe. Perhaps she could even help him with some of his work. How uncouth would it be if he not only showed up on her doorstep uninvited, but brought his work along with him? But at least it would keep him occupied if she refused to let him inside.

His butler appeared in the door.

"Lady Harding." Rafferty stepped aside revealing Sophia, her eyes narrowed, lips pursed.

CHAPTER SEVENTEEN

"Is something wrong?" Camden asked.

Sophia blinked. Apparently she needed to work on the whole wanton, seductress look. "I need to speak to you."

"That will be all, Rafferty," Camden said. He pulled off his spectacles and set them on the desk next to him. "You didn't come here on your own, did you?" He strode to her side, taking her shoulders in his hands and twisting her slightly as if inspecting her for injuries. At least he was touching her. This was a step in the right direction.

Even if he looked like he wanted to throttle her.

"Concerned for your virtue?" She tried to lighten the intensity in his expression, but when it didn't work, she sighed. Yes, a fine coquette she made. "The coachman and two grooms accompanied me. All armed."

"In a closed carriage or open?"

"Open. The coach has a broken axle, if you recall."

"You cannot—"

"No." She cut him off before he spoke the words she could not forgive. "I make my own decisions. I will not be ordered."

Camden's brows drew together. "I only want you safe."

"Because I'm too weak to protect myself?"

"No, because I care about you."

He spoke softly yet each of his words planted deep within her, rooting in the places she'd feared dead. The remnants of her anger drained. Camden had been trying to do his duty. That was nothing like Richard. Was she going to fight against breathing just because Richard had breathed too?

Camden's thumbs rubbed slow circles on her shoulders, robbing her knees of strength and reigniting the longing that had driven her here in the first place. She'd wanted to see him again, craved it like the girl lurking outside her brother's lesson. Did that mean she'd managed to save some of her innocence from Richard?

But the feelings twisting in her chest were anything but innocent.

She traced her hands up over his shoulders, lingering over the broad strength and the hard muscles before twining them behind his neck.

She could hear his rough swallow, felt it ripple along his throat.

"Why are you here, Sophia?"

"You said to come when I was sure." She walked to the door and pushed it closed, then returned and rose on her tiptoes to press a kiss to the line of his jaw. "I'm certain now. This is what I want."

"When I said we'd wait until you were certain, I was anticipating it taking more than a few hours."

"I'm ready for this." She'd been ready for this moment since she was fifteen.

But when he backed away for the third time that day, she almost staggered from the blow. "If you don't want me, tell me outright. Apparently, I don't take hints well."

He wrapped his arm around her waist before she could escape. "I want you."

"Then why are you backing away?"

"Because I want more from you than this." His hand dropped to caress her breast, but then it stilled over her heart. "I want this, too."

She was the one who took the step back this time, breaking his hold.

"I—" She retreated again, the back of her thighs colliding against the desk. She put her hand down to catch her balance and froze when she saw what she touched.

"My letter." She picked it up, tracing her finger over the curvy, girlish script. When he hadn't replied she'd preferred to assume it had become lost somewhere in the middle of the English Channel. But he *had* received it.

"Why did you keep it?"

A flush inched up his cheeks. "It was the only letter I received."

"The only love letter."

"No. The only letter."

She stared at him. "Your father—"

"Never wanted me to waste my intellectual talents by going to war. But how could I stay home with my head buried in numbers when I could be saving lives with them? He never agreed. Mathematics should be pristine. Theory alone. Practical application taints me."

"But you're working for your father, aren't you?"

"Solving this problem was simply a side interest of mine until he decided to pit Ipswith, his golden boy, in a race against me. He thinks I've wasted my talent helping out Thorp with his locomotive design. Or the city of Grundton with plans for their new well. My failure is his way of proving it. I thought perhaps if I beat Ipswith, I could convince some of the mathematicians to join me."

"Do you think they will? It sounds quite noble."

He gingerly took the letter from her fingers. "It also pays well. I'd hoped my success would sway them." He dropped his eyes to the letter, but not before she recognized loneliness, a bitter sore that had wounded his young heart. "So you see, I rather liked the idea that someone cared whether I lived or died." He folded the paper with practiced ease.

She closed the distance between them, her finger rasping over the rough stubble on his chin. "I did care. I still do."

Dropping the letter back on the desk, Camden's lips claimed hers, bold, fierce. No hesitation. "See, I'm not noble," he whispered. "I'm trying to have all these good intentions. Yet I say the say the things that I know will draw you to my side. Bring the words of affection I crave to your lips."

His hand stroked her breast, robbing her of the ability to respond. Besides, he was giving her what she'd come here for. Nothing else mattered. Heart thrumming in her ears, she dragged his head back down until she could reach his lips, exploring them as his hands explored her body.

The books for her library could be forgotten; she'd fill her life with this. With him.

Her blood sped so furiously through her veins that colors swirled at the edges of her vision, but she kept her eyes open, not wanting to miss a single moment as she unbuttoned his waistcoat and tugged his shirt free, slipping her hands underneath to the hard planes of his chest. Her hand slowed over his heart. Did he love her, then? She moved her hand and pressed her lips against that spot, reveling in the warmth and vibrancy in his hot, firm skin.

After she'd married Richard, she'd spent months trying to make him love her. It was heady and freeing to think that Camden might love her, not because she'd pandered and scraped but because she was herself.

But then his fingers found her nipple, gently rolling it, and her musings scattered.

So different. With Richard it had been all about trying to please him, to keep him happy, at least while she still bothered to try.

But this . . . *This.*

Camden gave as much as he took. His eyes never left hers as he caressed her, watching her as she watched him. Gauging her pleasure, driving it higher. But there was something more in his expression, a tenderness. As if she were precious and he couldn't bear to look away.

His fingers danced over her breasts, her neck, her face. When he his mouth followed, it was too much and at the same time not enough. She'd been married three years. How could her body react so differently to this man?

She shoved his jacket from his shoulders, wanting him bared, wanting to ignore the question she'd just asked herself.

He let his coat slip to the floor, then helped her lift his shirt over her head. She stopped for a moment, unable to do anything but relish the sight of him. She'd mourned as the days turned into weeks without a response to her letter. She'd finally given up, heartbroken and resigned to the fact that he would never be hers. But now he was. At least for the night. All of him was hers to claim. The thickly muscled shoulders that tapered to a ridged, narrow abdomen.

Unable to resist, she laid a kiss again to the center of his chest, loving the rapid intake of breath pressing his skin more tightly against her lips. His fingers tucked under her chin, lifting her face to his. Her name on his lips sweetened the caress.

She'd been lying when she told herself having him in her bed might satisfy her. Now that she had him, she wouldn't give him up. Perhaps deep within, her heart had never intended to.

Suddenly she didn't know where to look. She couldn't hold his gaze. She wasn't ready for him to see what she'd discovered, yet she was afraid if she closed her eyes, she'd no longer know where she ended and he began.

So she settled for the waistband of his trousers. She fumbled with the buttons there, her attempts slowed by the temptation to run her fingers up and down the length of him. Finally, she focused long enough to free the buttons and take him in her hand.

Camden's hands dug into her shoulders. "We can be in my room in less than a minute."

She had to speak between gasps. "Too long."

With only a brief pause, Camden locked the door, scooped her into his arms, and carried her over to the fireplace. When he would have laid her on the rug, she shook her head. "The desk. You have no idea how many times I pictured us there last night."

Camden cleared the desk with a single sweep of his arm. The ink bottle flew through the air and clattered onto the rug. He hoped it remained stoppered.

He set Sophia on her feet, turning her away from him so he could have access to her buttons. Whose idea was it to have so many buttons on dresses?

Her breathless chuckle trembled under his fingers. "You should write a paper on the ability of buttons to multiply exponentially."

Camden couldn't help his chuckle any more than he could help the fierce exaltation at sharing the jest with her. "Ipswith could not compete with that."

She'd admitted she cared for him. While that was nothing compared to the depth of his feelings, it was enough to ignite hope that he'd be able to earn more.

As the last button popped from its mooring, he slid the black dress from her shoulders, reveling in the dark fabric giving way to the creaminess of her skin. It pooled on the floor like the ink from the jar. Sophia kicked the garment away, leaving her clothed as she'd been this afternoon.

"You have no idea how the image of you dressed like this has tormented me." Camden's fingers shook slightly as he unlaced her stays. "How much I regretted not finishing things."

"It's only been a few hours."

"I know. I will be forever grateful you rescued me in time to save most of my mental faculties."

She tipped her head back onto his shoulder, jutting her breasts up for his view. "Only most?"

"Indeed. Coherent sentences seem to . . . escape me."

She turned toward him. With one fluid motion, she pulled off her shift and let it slip from her fingers. "You can still form sentences?"

No longer. Perfection—slender and delicate, yet sweetly curved. Pale skin. Soft like sweet silk. Camden lowered his mouth to the tip of one breast to sample the peaked, rosy nipple.

Her hissed breath ended in a throaty moan.

He loved this, the pleasuring of her. There was simplicity in such an action. Two separate variables joining to create a rational solution. He'd made love to other women, but never had there been this completeness. Like he'd restored a piece of himself long missing.

He lowered his hand to the softness between her legs, his body clenching at the wet, molten heat that met his fingers. He gently parted her folds, pleasuring her until she bucked wildly in his arms. He took each motion, each sound, and tucked it deep in his heart. The knowledge of her pleasure drove his own until he groaned with the impossible intensity.

Her head tipped back and she cried out his name. She arched against him as she climaxed, her breath coming in ragged gasps. In that moment, he gently caught her chin, holding her gaze. Her eyes were wide, unguarded, vulnerable, yet she didn't look away.

Camden forgot how to breathe. He forgot everything but the connection burning between them.

But then her head dropped to his chest, breaking the bond. He traced his lips down the side of her neck, not willing to let her go.

Her head lifted, her expression wary as if her more rational self hadn't decided whether to trust him. But her passion was unchanged. "Shall we try the desk?"

Before he could answer, she'd lifted herself onto the edge and spread her legs, drawing him between her knees, stroking him until it took every ounce of self-control he had to keep sane.

Her teeth bit her lower lip when he caressed up and down her inner thighs. "Please, I want—"

He paused there at her slick entrance, allowing himself only small teasing movements, tormenting them both. "Want what?" He didn't know what he'd do if she said she just wanted to see if she could make love to someone. He'd seen more than that in her gaze. He needed her to be willing to admit it.

Yet despite all his pride, he didn't think he'd be strong enough to back away no matter her answer.

"I want you, Camden. I want all of you."

That was close enough to what he needed to hear. Camden plunged forward, claiming the ecstasy of her body. He tried to slow his movements, but she wouldn't let him, lying back on the desk, her legs wrapping around his waist, urging him on.

"I love you," he whispered. She might not be ready to hear the words, but he had to speak them. Loving her with his body couldn't be separated from loving her with his soul.

When he dropped his hand to the place where their bodies joined, she cried out again. "I think I've always loved you" was the reply he heard before his body lost to the brutal release that thundered through him, deluging every nerve ending with utter satisfaction.

Chapter Eighteen

Sophia sat snuggled in Camden's lap in his chair in front of the desk.

"I may never be able to do a single proof at that desk again." His lips moved against the sensitive spot below her ear.

She traced a finger down the bridge of his nose. "Have any other places I can ruin?"

He nipped her lightly. "I never said you ruined it. In fact, I was thinking of having it preserved as a shrine to perfection."

She rested her head on his chest, not daring to speak anymore. She had no idea what she'd say if he questioned her about what she'd confessed.

She'd said she loved him.

Was it true? It felt true. When she had said the words, everything broken in her life had suddenly seemed whole.

But was it really? Did those words really have that power or did she just want them to?

A man stomped in the corridor, clearing his throat loudly.

"I think your butler wishes to speak to you."

Camden circled her nipple with his thumb. "We can ignore him."

She barely stopped a moan. "We'll have to leave the room at some point. I find I'm quite hungry."

Camden lifted her from his lap, smoothing his hand down her side. "I meant what I said. I love you, Sophia."

She caught his hand, brushing her lips across the ink stains that she found so intriguing, hoping he'd understand her acceptance and not press her more. "Do you see my shift?"

After several rushed, giggling moments they managed to dress and sit by the desk. Not that she doubted that anyone looking at them wouldn't know exactly what they'd done, but at least this way she might be able to manage looking Rafferty in the eye again.

Someday.

His knock was light on the door. "Sir, I hate to disturb you during your . . . work. But the Runner claims he needs to speak to you urgently. There is something amiss with the investigation."

When they entered the parlor, Williamson was pacing back and forth in front of the fire. "I can't find the gardener."

"He wasn't with Mrs. Haws?" Camden asked.

An icy fear filled Sophia's chest. "I saw him a few hours ago. He said he was going to deliver the list to you."

Williamson shook his head. "He didn't. And he never returned to your house. I checked with your servants."

Sophia's hands shook. "Something must have happened to him. Perhaps you missed each other. Took separate paths." Her hands pressed against her cheeks. "What if he was harmed by an attack meant for me?"

Williamson tapped his fingers on his leg. "Or he was responsible for your attacks and he's running."

"Impossible. He's always protected me." She stiffened her spine. "We have to find him."

Camden was already in the corridor, calling for his coach.

"You said you saw the list," Williamson said. "Can you recreate it for me? If something has happened to him, it could be tied to one of the women on the list."

"I think so." She hurried to the side table and wrote the names down, at least the ones she could remember. But she might be missing someone.

Camden's hand settled on her shoulder. "We know Wicken was headed for town. We'll go there first. We can double check your list with Mrs. Haws's."

Fifteen minutes later, they were rattling toward the center of the village. As soon as the carriage stopped, Sophia leapt down without waiting for assistance. She ran into the tavern with Camden close behind her.

"Sweet mercy, what is it, child?" Mrs. Haws paused, a pitcher of ale above the tankard of one of her customers.

"More ale!" someone else shouted from the other side of the room.

"I can't be in two places at once, now, can I?" Mrs. Haws glared. "Sorry, my lady. I'm a bit short on help today."

"Wicken. Have you seen him?"

She shook her head. "No. The Runner was looking for him, too. Did he not find him?"

Sophia shook her head and pulled out the paper. "Are these all the names on the list you both made?"

Mrs. Haws took the paper and squinted at it. "I think so.

No, wait. Lottie. My serving girl. She's missing. From the list and from my tavern."

Sophia's head swam. Only Camden's hands on her waist steadied her.

"What is it?" he asked Sophia. "Do you know anything about Lottie?"

"She's Wicken's daughter. And I didn't leave her name off the list. It wasn't on the one he showed me."

CHAPTER NINETEEN

Lottie's cottage was dark as they approached. Even in the dwindling twilight, the perfectly kept vegetables and lush roses clearly showed Wicken's touch. But there was no sign of anyone.

Camden knocked on the door.

No answer.

He peered in one of the windows but could see nothing in the darkness.

"We still don't know what this means," Sophia said.

Camden tightened his arm around her shoulders and kept silent.

But Williamson had no such qualms. "He's probably long fled with his family." He sniffed the air. "There hasn't been a fire at this house today."

"I won't believe him guilty until I have proof."

Williamson snorted. "I'll check around back."

A sharp pain exploded in Camden's shoulder. "What the devil?" He shoved Sophia behind him as another rock bounced off his chest. "Who—"

There was a thump and then sounds of a scuffle around the edge of the house. "Williamson might need help. Stay here," he told Sophia.

But when he ran toward the sounds of the struggle, Sophia was right behind him.

"Let me go, you bloody bastard," shouted a young voice.

Camden halted barely in time to keep from colliding with Williamson, who was coming around the corner, a lad restrained in front of him.

"This is the boy who was throwing rocks. Know him?"

The boy's face was hard to see in the darkness, but then he turned fully toward her and she gasped. "This is Lottie's son, Lewis. Wicken's grandson."

The boy struggled against Williamson. "Like you don't know who else I am. Like you don't know the person you robbed."

Sophia tipped her head and spoke softly. "I'm afraid I don't know what you're speaking of."

The boy spat. "You whore."

That Camden would have none of. He stepped in front of the boy. "If you speak to Lady Harding that way again there will be consequences."

"How about the consequences she should get for stealing my inheritance?" But some of the bluster had left the lad, making him seem younger, frailer.

"Perhaps you should explain," Sophia said.

The boy glowered. "As if you don't know. My father always told me I'd be living with him, except you wouldn't let me."

"What does Lady Harding have to do with your father?" Williamson asked.

But the pieces suddenly fell in place for Camden, and he knew from Sophia's inhale that she'd realized the same thing.

Lord Harding had been his father. Camden could see it now in the coloring of the boy's hair and his slight build.

"He promised he'd set money aside for me, money that you couldn't touch. The estate was settled last week. Where is my money?" The boy's voice cracked. "It's not like you need it."

"You were behind the attacks on Lady Harding," Camden said.

The boy thrashed suddenly. "Why shouldn't I? She killed him. She killed my father. My grandfather told me you'd come to investigate her."

It was *his* fault the attacks had been directed at her, but Camden tucked that stab of guilt away to apologize for later. "You tried to kill her for revenge."

The boy's eyes were wide in the moonlight. "No. I tried to scare her. Let her know that I wasn't going to give up my money without a fight."

"You shot at her."

"I shot above her head. And tried to frighten her with the other things. But she didn't even care. It's my money. It might not seem a lot to you, but it's a fortune to me."

Sophia's hands clasped tightly in front of her. "There was no money for you in the will. I did not even know you were Lord Harding's son until now."

"Lies!" the boy cried, his hair falling over his eyes. "He told me how you, so high and mighty, were embarrassed by his bastard."

Camden tried to feel compassion for the boy, but it was difficult. Any of his acts could have hurt Sophia. "Your father only married Lady Harding three years ago. If he was going to claim you, why didn't he do it?"

Sophia, of course, did what she could to protect the boy and soften the truth. "Lord Harding told people what he wanted them to believe. To make himself look good. He lied to many people. Even to me. I'm sorry."

The boy paused, tears glistening in his eyes, but then he spat. "You killed him."

"Trying to cast blame?" Williamson asked. "Did you get tired of waiting for your money? Did you get bitter at him and his wife for the wrongs you thought she did you?"

"It wasn't Lewis. Let him go." Wicken stepped out of the darkness into the garden. "I killed Harding."

Sophia stared at the older man, willing him to take the words back. But he stood resolute, his chin lifted, aged shoulders squared. It had been Wicken after all, he—

A thought occurred to her. "Tubs said the killer was hired by a woman."

Wicken ducked his head. "He must have been mistaken. I hired the man—"

"Two men," Sophia corrected.

Wicken rubbed his arm. "I did. You hear me, Lord Grey. You and the constable can arrest me and take me away."

"No." A third voice spoke. A woman's voice. Lottie came to stand beside her father. Her hair was concealed in a kerchief and a shawl was around her shoulders.

"Lottie, Lewis is back. Just take him and leave like we'd planned."

The woman hugged her arms tightly around her. "It was me, Da. I think you've always known it."

"Lottie—"

"No. You can't protect me any longer."

The boy broke away from Williamson and threw himself at his mother, his bony arms wrapping around her waist. "It was Lady Harding. It was."

Lottie rested her cheek on the top of her son's head. "I wouldn't let him ruin you, too. I couldn't let his lies hurt you."

"But they weren't lies. The money—"

"There was no money. He never had any intention of claiming you, not even when he demanded you quit your apprenticeship with the blacksmith. When I confronted him about it, he went wild with rage. He didn't want his son dirtied in trade but he wouldn't give a cent to provide for you. He beat me. I couldn't take the chance that someday he'd hurt you, too." She looked up at Sophia then, the horror and pain in her eyes finding a perfect echo inside her.

If she had a child, she might have done the same thing.

"No!" the boy shouted, his shoulders jerking.

"He broke Grandda's arm."

"He said it was an accident. He—"

"He broke your grandfather's arm because Lord Harding was trying to hurt me," Sophia said.

"You must have deserved it."

Camden, Williamson, and Wicken all started to protest, but she cut them off. "No. I did not." The truth in her words sunk deep, flinging open a darkly shuttered corner of her soul that she didn't know still existed.

You have to think you're worth protecting, Camden had said.

Her voice gained strength as she spoke. "Your father was a cruel, insecure man. He failed us all. But the way he decided to act wasn't my fault. It wasn't your mother's fault and it wasn't yours."

Lewis buried his face in his mother's bosom, sobs wracking his body. Wicken took them both in his arms, tears tracking down his cheeks.

"What do you want me to do, sir?" Williamson asked. "Do you want to press charges against the boy or just the mother?"

Wicken turned toward them, putting his family behind him, shielding them as he had her.

"How many more lives does Richard have to ruin?" she asked Camden.

His hand briefly clasped hers, then he stepped away. "Come with me around the side of the cottage to the coach, Williamson. I have rope inside. As a justice of the peace, I must act."

"Shouldn't I—"

"Come, Williamson. They'll only be out of sight for a moment."

And Sophia realized what he was letting her do.

Williamson's eyes narrowed, but he followed.

"Go," Sophia said as soon as Camden was around the corner.

"My lady?" Wicken asked.

"Go, now. Disappear."

Wicken walked to her side, a gnarled finger wiping away a tear she didn't know was on her cheek.

"Go."

"I damn Lord Harding, but I will bless you forever, my

lady. I swear I'll watch over them. Nothing like this will be allowed to happen again." With a slow shuffle, he led his family into the darkness.

Camden and Williamson returned with a rope.

Williamson swore. "You let a killer go free."

Camden lifted a brow. "It's unfortunate they escaped." But his arms wrapped around her waist, his hands tender.

Williamson shook his head in resignation. "I don't suppose you'll tell me which direction they went, my lady?"

"It was too dark."

Williamson glanced around. "I suppose I must search so I can report I gave chase." He grumbled and disappeared into the darkness, in the opposite direction Wicken had chosen.

Sophia threw her arms around Camden, pressing a kiss to his throat. "Thank you."

He cupped her chin, his lips finding her mouth. "I have no idea what you mean. I'll have to tell everyone I was eluded by an old man, a woman, and a boy."

A moan whispered from her throat as he deepened the kiss, his tongue sweeping over hers. But she knew with a sinking certainty what she must do.

"I love you," she said.

Camden lifted his head long enough to grin. "I— What's wrong?"

She took a deep breath. She was worth protecting, she reminded herself. And she was worth waiting for. "I love you, but there are parts of me that are not as healed as I thought. I want to make you happy, so much it scares me. I love you, but I said it last night because I knew it would please you, not because I was ready. You were right, I need time."

A crease slashed his brow. "I was a fool. Don't listen to me."

"I need to protect myself." She owed it to Camden. She owed it to herself.

He swallowed. "What do you need to do?"

"I have nine months left of my mourning. I'm going to leave Weltford. Travel. Do whatever I wish. See my family, perhaps. I've been avoiding them, you know. I could not face them."

"You have nothing to be ashamed of." He said it with such conviction that her heart clenched. It almost changed her mind.

"I believed that before. But I didn't *know* that until now."

"Stay here," he said. "I'll give you whatever space you need."

She took a deep breath, drawing in the scents of the garden to steady her. The damp soil. The roses. And Camden. "But I don't know if I could stay away from you. If I was here, I couldn't stop from giving you everything I am. And I can't do that until I am woman I want to give."

The lines of Camden's face were stark in the moonlight, his eyes shadowed. "Will you return to me?"

"I hope so."

"I'll wait."

Sophia stood on tiptoe again and pulled his lips to hers for one final kiss. He met it with searing ferocity, his lips branding her. She returned the intensity, marking him as hers.

Finally, they parted, panting. She trailed her finger across his lips, needing one final touch even as she knew that would never be enough. "Make sure you write me back this time."

CHAPTER TWENTY

Dear Sophia,

Regarding your recent epistle, yes, I have heard of his works. It is an intriguing notion to use the theorem. I shall have to try it.

I had a letter from father this morning informing me that Ipswith was not as close to the discovery as he thought. The society meeting has been postponed a month. Which is fortuitous, given that I am no closer either.

Rafferty enquired this morning why I've taken to working in the library rather than at the desk in my study. I simply told him it was far easier to keep my thoughts on my work if I was in the library.

An equation I was working on the other day had infinite solutions. I found myself wishing I had that many words for telling you of my love, but all I could think of was the soft sigh of your breath against my throat as you nestled on my lap.

Camden

"You still have a few minutes, but we will need to hurry if we are to dress for the poetry reading," Sophia's mother said. Even though Sophia had been wandering through Frotnam's bookshop for over an hour, her mother had not fidgeted once. Her younger sister, Claire, on the other hand, had walked up and down every row, pulled out and replaced a dozen books, and quizzed the owner on the best methods for dealing with mold.

Sophia stood in the first row, reading title after title, her arms still empty. Her finger trailed over the cool, gleaming leather. "I will stay here a while longer."

"We can return tomorrow. Or you can have a bit longer if you need and we can arrive late." Her mother sent Claire a look to silence her groan.

Sophia rested her hand against the shelf, finding power in the oak. "Please, go on without me. I have no particular fondness for poetry readings."

Her mother patted her shoulder. "I'm sure if you come, you will enjoy yourself. You had a lovely time at the musicale last night."

"Yes, I did, but I don't wish to go tonight."

"I know you sometimes feel shy, but surely if you tried—"

Sophia released her hold on the shelf. She didn't need it for strength. She took both her mother's hands in hers. "I know you love these events, but I do not. I never have. I do enjoy going and seeing my friends, but it drains me. I find one or two events a week more than enough. Besides, I spent most of the afternoon touring Sir Reginald's new exhibit at the museum with Bennett and Mari. I haven't been lacking company."

Her mother blinked. "You'd truly prefer to stay home?"

Sophia nodded, secretly exalted that she'd finally refused, yet bracing for the argument she knew would come.

But instead, her mother clasped her hands tightly. "I have not done well with you, have I?" Sophia started to speak but her mother cut her off. "No, I haven't. Growing up with your father and I cannot have been easy. We adore being out in the bustle of society. I thought I was encouraging you to love life as we do. But you have found your own way to love it." She brushed a light kiss on Sophia cheek. "I will respect that. Come, Claire."

Her younger sister was, for once, speechless as her mother dragged her from the shop.

"I will send the coach back for you." The bell above the door jingled as they exited.

She'd done it. She yanked the nearest book from the shelf and clutched it to her chest, the pasteboard corners digging into her palms. She could hear her mother's coach clattering away down the cobblestone street.

And she didn't feel guilty.

But as she waited, book heavy in her arms, she didn't feel any different either. A trifle stronger, happier, but not different.

In fact, nothing she'd done over the past six months had made her different. Her heart had healed more from Richard's abuse. She'd rediscovered parts of herself, but nothing had transformed her.

She'd rather thought this step would.

Yet she was happy. Or at least, content. She didn't think

she'd be happy until she could return to Camden in another three months.

She stared at the book she had chosen, a treatise on mathematical innovation. Perhaps she could send it to him, although she'd much prefer to read it with him. But that would have to wait.

She studied the gilt words imprinted on the cover. Were the expectations of society the only reason she was waiting? Why couldn't she manage to escape them?

Because that wasn't who she was.

She knew in that instant what the flaw had been in her thinking all along. She could grow and strengthen, but in the end she'd always be—herself.

She selected two more books and then hurried to the counter to pay for her purchases.

CHAPTER TWENTY-ONE

Camden stood in his father's crowded drawing room. Ip-swith's success had drawn out members he hadn't seen in years, curious to see the man's solution. But Ipswith had kept a very tight rein on his paper thus far. No one had seen it. No one could claim to have verified it.

Camden almost hadn't come, but he had to see the answer. True, he'd been distracted over the past six months—checking for the post every hour in case Sophia had replied to his latest letter, beating his butler to the door every time he heard hoof beats—but something about the concept still didn't fit right.

A hand clapped him on the back. "If you hadn't been cork-brained enough to join the army, that could be you about to deliver the paper." His father's gut had grown since Camden had last seen him and his jowls hung heavier on his chin, but the look of pious judgment on his face was the same. "Your title didn't improve your wits, it would seem."

The disapproval didn't sting as it once had. Sophia thought his work noble. Nothing his father could fling at him could touch that. "My mathematics didn't suffer for my service to the Crown." It had him stronger, more disciplined, but he kept silent. His father always believed what he chose.

"What about your well-digging and factory-building? If you'd spent more time pursuing more pure goals, you'd—"

"Not be the fascinating genius he is now."

Sophia.

She stood beside them, dressed in a lavender gown that skimmed low across her bosom and highlighted a healthy glow in her cheeks. He hadn't seen her in that color in a long time. It made her appear younger and more innocent. And altogether delectable.

Camden suddenly realized just how little he cared about this meeting or the fact that the chairmanship was about to go to his rival. His heart hammered against his ribs and he slid his finger along the satin of her cheek to make sure she was real.

His father drew back shocked, but Sophia smiled, pressing her cheek into his caress.

"Lady Sophia Harding, may I present my father, Mr. Lucas Grey. Father, Lady Sophia Harding."

Sophia dipped into a perfect curtsey, but barely glanced at his father.

Why was she here? He had three months left to wait. Well, eighty-nine days if he'd been tracking things that closely.

For the first time that evening, he wished he'd solved the theorem first, so Sophia could have found him in his moment of triumph. But being the loser definitely had its advantages— like being able to leave when he desired.

Such as now.

He clasped Sophia's hand tightly in his and pulled her from the room. After three tries, he found an empty parlor and pulled her into it, shutting the door and locking it behind him. Her hands twined around his neck, her lips seeking his before his hand had left the handle.

With a groan, he crushed her to him, running his hands down her back to the soft perfection of her hips. She tasted of sugar and cream and happiness. Her hands clenched tightly in his hair, holding him close. She backed him to the settee, pushing him down. "I missed you," she whispered, straddling him.

He clung to his only remaining thread of sanity as he sank into the soft cushions. "Why are you here?"

She slid off his lap to sit next to him. "I've had an epiphany." A smile curved her lips, tempered with a confidence stronger than when he'd last seen her.

"Three months early?" he asked, exploring the outline of her lips.

"That is part of it. I wrote you of that in my letters, my silly explorations."

Camden hadn't thought them silly. He'd cheered, perhaps embarrassingly loud, at her exploits in her letters. Much to the worry of his servants.

"I found that while I'll never be the belle of the ball, I'm good at making close friends and keeping them. I found that I like novels but not poetry. I found I like staying in my room with a good book rather than dragging myself to every event my family invites me to. I found I actually like some events if I get to select them."

She leaned forward, her hands on his chest, her face hovering above his. A tendril of her hair had escaped her pins and caressed his cheek. "After I left, I kept seeking some great transformation. For the key that would unlock the perfect version of who I should have been."

His heart hammered in his chest. He wanted to pull her to him and whisper all the beautiful things about her, but he knew that he needed to be silent and listen.

"But then I realized, I don't need a transformation. There is nothing wrong with me. What I needed to discover was the strength to accept everything I am—and am not. What I needed to learn these past months was how to make the right choices for me and not be ashamed of them." Her lips brushed his. "And you are right for me. And that will be true now. In three months. And forever. I love you."

"I. Love. You." He punctuated each word with a kiss. "Then you won't leave again? Because I'm not sure I can let you go a second time."

"I'm staying."

With a growl of triumph, he crushed his mouth to hers. "Marry me?" His heart stuttered as he awaited her answer. He hadn't pushed her too fast, had he? Perhaps he should have given her a few days. But he'd been waiting six months to say the words and now that she was here, they refused to be constrained.

Her eyes lit with utter bliss. "Yes."

This time his kiss was slow. He feathered it over her lips, her jaw, drawing out this moment now that he had an infinite amount of them.

But she was mistaken. She was perfect. Her imperfection was perfection.

Then he stilled, the thoughts that had been disarrayed in

his head slowly snapping into place. Perfection didn't exist within his equation either. That's why he couldn't find the solution.

"Camden?"

"You *are* my muse." He hugged her, thoughts still settling. "Can you help me find paper?"

She nodded and helped him scour the room until they found paper and ink in a lady's writing desk.

He filled the page with numbers. Then another page. He was right. He tossed down the paper. "Ipswith is either a liar or wrong because he didn't find a generic way to solve the equations. There is no general formula. None. And I can prove why."

Sophia handed him a fresh sheet of paper and he outlined his thoughts and evidence, explaining how the lower-degree polynomial equations had a structure to their roots that the quintics lacked. Quintics were a mass of glorious imperfection.

Through the closed door, he could hear the applause signaling the start of Ipswith's presentation.

"Go," Sophia urged. "Show them."

He finally had it. He could stride into the room and make his father and Ipswith look like fools, make himself look like a genius.

But that wouldn't change his father's opinion.

He folded the paper over, wrote his father's name on it, and stood, leaving it on the desk. A servant would find it and give it to his father in the morning.

Camden pulled Sophia to him. "The only solution I care about is the one I'm holding in my arms."

Can't get enough of Anna Randol?
Read on for excerpts from her previous novel,
A Secret in Her Kiss,
and her upcoming book,
Sins of a Virgin,
on sale 8/28/12 from Avon Books
wherever e-books are sold!

An Excerpt from
A SECRET IN HER KISS

Chapter One

Belgium, 1815

The last of the supply barrels thudded into the weathered rowboat.

The leather-faced sailor tugged at the edge of his knit cap. "Be back for ye and yers in a few ticks, sir."

Major Bennett Prestwood nodded, and the man cast off the thick rope securing the boat to the dock. The oars scraped along the side of the boat, then dipped into the water, trailing ripples behind as the sailor rowed the supplies toward the navy frigate anchored in the bay.

Bennett flicked his hand, scattering two seagulls who'd settled on his trunk. It was perhaps a bit lowering to be loaded after the salted beef, but if it meant passage back to England, he'd be content to be loaded after the wharf rats.

He drew a deep breath. The docks of Ostend stank. They stank of fish and filth. He inhaled again. But the breeze didn't reek of decaying human flesh covered in lye. And it didn't carry the screams of the wounded.

For a few hours, he was on leave from hell. No graves to dig. No armies to scout. No enemies to kill.

But when he reached England, his respite would be over.

Bennett growled to himself, frightening an old beggar woman seeking alms or pockets to pick or perhaps both. He tossed the remainder of his money into her chipped clay cup. He'd be home soon enough.

Then he'd kill his brother-in-law.

Bennett's hand tightened on the smooth leather hilt of his sword, worn down until he could feel the cool metal underneath. He was supposed to be finished with this. He'd intended to leave death buried with the corpses of his fallen men in the muddy fields of Waterloo.

But then his mother had sent him a letter.

He rubbed the grit from his face and withdrew the creased paper from his pocket. His mother had chatted on in her charming way about the normal family gossip. His younger brother had been sent down from Eton again. His cousins were leaving on a Grand Tour. His sister, Sophia, had reconciled with her husband and returned to his estate. Bennett's jaw clenched as he read that final line for the hundredth time. He crumpled the paper and threw it into the harbor. He no longer needed it. The sentence had burned itself into his mind.

Damnation, why hadn't he sent her farther away? She'd be better off in the wilds of India than with the bastard she'd married.

How had her husband forced her back? Another broken rib? A promise he would keep only until he was in his cups again?

If she couldn't stay away from him, Bennett would see to it that her husband stayed away from her.

A large ebony coach rattled to a halt in front of him, blocking his view of the ship. Bennett tensed, his hand again sliding to the sword at his waist.

The coach door opened. "Join me a moment, Prestwood."

Bennett's jaw locked at that nasal voice. Curse it all, not now. "What do you want, General?"

"A simple word with you."

A lie. General Caruthers was army intelligence; nothing was ever simple with him.

"That's an order, Prestwood."

Bennett climbed into the dimness of the coach. Caruthers smiled at him, the expression stretching the soft, pasty dough of his face. "Care for a drink, Major?" He pulled two glasses from a compartment in the wall of the coach.

"No."

Caruthers poured some brandy into his glass from a silver flask. "This is why I never stole you away from your regiment. No skill for putting others at ease."

He didn't want to be at ease. He needed to be on that ship.

"But you always follow orders, and that's a trait I find useful."

Dread settled in Bennett's gut as the general removed a sheet of paper from a folio next to him and smoothed it on his lap with near reverence. He handed it to Bennett.

Bennett held the page at arm's length, loath to involve himself with more of Caruthers's nonsense. Yet the sheet caught his attention regardless. The paper didn't contain orders. "It's a butterfly."

The general nodded and his jowls bounced enthusiastically. "Exactly! That's the genius of it. Look closer."

A pounding ache built at the base of Bennett's skull. He wanted nothing more to do with secrets and lies. Yet since the man outranked him, he peered intently.

Nothing changed. The butterfly was still just a glorified insect, albeit skillfully wrought in ink. In fact, more than skillfully. Bennett held the drawing up in the hazy square of afternoon light that filtered through the thick glass windows. The delicate creature poised on a branch and looked, for all the world, as if it would flutter away at any moment. How had the artist done it? Bennett twisted the paper from side to side and still couldn't discover the artist's trick.

Caruthers smiled smugly. "You'll never find it."

Bennett lowered the paper, grateful for the general's misinterpretation of his prolonged study.

Caruthers's fingers dug indents into his pudgy legs and his eyes gleamed.

Bennett sighed and ventured into the noose. "Very well. Tell me what is special about this particular butterfly." He laid the drawing flat on his knee.

The general traced a small section of lines near the tip of the wing. "It's in the wings. Here." He reached under his seat, pulled out a large glass magnifier, and held it over the drawing.

"Bloody hell." Under the enlargement of the glass, minuscule lines came into focus, lines that unmistakably outlined the specifications and defenses of a military fortification. "Where is this?"

"A new Ottoman fort near the Greek border city of Ainos on the Mediterranean."

"How did he get this information?"

Discomfort marred the general's face and he cleared his throat. "Not a he. A she. It's recently come to our attention that the artist is, in fact, a woman."

Bennett folded his arms. "How exactly did His Majesty's government succeed in missing that small detail?"

General Caruthers coughed twice. "Well, it appears that the government's man in Constantinople assumed the woman delivering the drawings to be the artist's servant rather than the artist."

"Who is she? A Greek patriot?"

The general's face sank into annoyed lines and he plucked at a brass button on his sleeve. "As a matter of fact, it has recently come to light that she is British. One Mari Sinclair."

An Englishwoman? Why wasn't she safe in England where she belonged? "What is she doing in the heart of the Ottoman Empire?" The Turks weren't kind to spies. And the tortures they could inflict on a female spy were infinitely worse.

"Her father is an archaeologist of minor renown, a Sir Reginald Sinclair. He excavates in the area."

Bennett tried to recall anything of the family but didn't recognize the name. He studied the drawing again. "If you don't mind my asking, sir, why are you showing me this?"

The general smiled. "You have done missions for us before."

Yes, he'd been assigned missions before, but those had been to eliminate enemies. The picture crinkled in Bennett's fist. "I do not kill women."

The general glared and retrieved the drawing before further damage befell it. "No, no. The opposite, in fact. Keep Miss Sinclair alive."

Definitely not Bennett's area of expertise. "Isn't this something better left to the Foreign Office? She's one of their agents, is she not?" The rowboat had begun its passage back to the dock, and he intended to be on it when it left. He needed to shake some sense into Sophia and, failing that, put a bullet through her husband's head.

"Actually, no. She's a naturalist who studies plants and insects and the like."

"She refused to work for them?" Perhaps the woman had an ounce of sense after all.

"She's a bit . . . independent. She just delivers the pictures when she desires." The general continued, "The Foreign Office has been providing a man to keep watch over her, but his protection is spotty at best. The army has interest in the drawings, so we informed the Foreign Office that we've arranged for her to work for us." He leaned in, a confidential tone coloring his words. "The Ottomans are falling apart from the inside. They're scrambling to build forts to hold on to Greece and their other territories, but they lack the funds to do so. Russia is kindly attempting to assist them."

Splendid. The fool woman had placed herself in the center of some political power struggle. "To what end?"

"Russia has long wanted a foothold in the Mediterranean. This arrangement leaves them perfectly poised if the Ottomans fall. We, of course, don't want to see this cozy little friendship succeed."

One thing still didn't make sense. "If she won't work for the Foreign Office, why has she agreed to work for us?"

Caruthers returned the glass to the box under his seat. "We've assured her that cooperation will be to her benefit."

Ah, benefit no doubt translated into gold. "Find someone else." He didn't have time to waste protecting a woman who thought money more important than safety.

Irritation leeched onto the general's face. "Impossible. You have something no one else does. A perfect cover."

Bennett raised his eyebrow.

"Your cousin is the ambassador assigned to Constantinople."

Damnation. Lord Henry Daller. The man was a dozen years older than Bennett. Bennett knew very little of him. "We don't have more than a passing acquaintance."

Caruthers shrugged. "But neither the Turks nor the Russians will question it when you arrive. A young gentleman out to see the Continent now that the war is finally over."

"What makes you think Miss Sinclair needs protection?"

The general struggled upright. "Her identity has been compromised."

"And she still insists on gathering information?" Bennett frowned. Then the woman was either addled or had a death wish—neither of which boded well for her survival.

"As I said, we've ensured her cooperation."

How much was the Crown paying her? But surely if her identity was known, the operation was as much at risk as her life. "Why not send another agent in her place?"

Caruthers rubbed his hands together eagerly. "She's been

able to access places we've only dreamed of before. We can't give her up."

"So we put her in danger."

"She's put herself in danger. Regardless, it's not for long. We only need two last areas."

Bennett stiffened. "This is ridiculous. I won't play with Miss Sinclair's life."

"You have no choice."

He already bore the guilt for failing to notice what was happening to Sophia; he wouldn't fling Miss Sinclair into further danger. He'd sacrificed most of his soul in the service of King and Country. He refused to surrender the rest. "I do have a choice. I resign my commission." He'd never expected to utter those words, but he would not let himself regret them.

Caruthers's lips puckered. "Unfortunate. I do regret that, although not as much as I regret what will befall Everston and O'Neil."

Bennett stilled. "What do my men have to do with this?"

"Everston lost a leg, did he not? And O'Neil an arm?"

Bennett swallowed the bile in his throat.

"It will be difficult for them to find work, I think. And poor O'Neil has three young children at home, too."

"What are you threatening?"

Caruthers rubbed his chin. "Threats? Tsk, tsk, Major. I'm merely stating how essential a pension will be for those injured men, and you know how fickle Parliament is. If for some reason your regiment were left off the list the army sends to Parliament for funding, it would be a great tragedy. It could take years to correct. How many in the Ninety-fifth Rifles are going to be relying on pensions?"

Too many. The rigorous dual roles of scout and sharp-shooter had decimated his men. Perhaps he could find positions for O'Neil and Everston on his estate, but what of the rest? He couldn't leave them to starve in the gutters. Caruthers would carry out his threat, too, and not lose a night's sleep.

"How long?" The question burned like acid on his lips.

Caruthers leaned back, the leather bench creaking under his weight. "I'm not asking for something unreasonable. We need Miss Sinclair to draw the two forts within the month. Then you are free to return to England."

A month. Bennett cast another glance at the dock. The sailor waited in the rowboat, his wrinkled face collapsed in confusion.

Curse it, Sophia. Why had he buckled under her sobbed pleas for secrecy? He'd given his word not to reveal the vile treatment she'd received at the hands of her husband. Now for another month, that promise left her at the mercy of the sadistic bastard.

"What are my orders?"

"Quite simple. Keep Miss Sinclair alive long enough to draw what I need."

"Sir, I—"

The general's expression sank into displeasure. "This is not a request, Major. You sail within the hour."

Bennett straightened and flung open the door to the coach. "Aye, sir."

Constantinople

Bennett studied the woman before him—or at least what little he could see—a grand total of two brown eyes. Not even her eyebrows showed under the garish golden silk that swathed her entire form. Her native garb stood in awkward contrast to the traditional English decor of the ambassador's parlor, clashing horribly with the pink embroidered flowers on the chair beneath her. A dandelion in one of his mother's rose beds. "So you agree to the conditions?"

Miss Sinclair dipped her head, shrinking even further into the overstuffed chair. "Yes," her words fluttered the fabric of her veil.

"I know it might be a bother to write out an hour-by-hour itinerary every morning, but it is for your safety."

"Yes, sir." She darted an anxious glance at the closed door.

Bennett paced in front of the large marble fireplace, then tapped his fingers on the mantel. Both of his sisters would've laughed in his face if he'd dared to make such a suggestion to one of them. He'd expected at least some protest. The sum the government was paying her must be substantial indeed.

Silence hung awkwardly in the stifling room. He eyed the shut windows. He still couldn't think of words to adequately describe the city of Constantinople spread out beneath them. The city resembled nothing so much as an aging courtesan's dressing room table overflowing with rouge pots and cream jars and a few candlesticks interspersed throughout.

He cleared his throat and forced his attention back to the woman in front of him. They could discuss the rest of his plans during the next few days. Now that they could claim an acquaintance, he could call on her without attracting undue attention. "That will be all for now, Miss Sinclair, it's been a pleasure to meet you."

She sprang to her feet in an eruption of silk and fled toward the door. Bennett scrambled to open it for her. The woman's work involved two of the most vindictive nations in Europe. He'd expected her to have more pluck.

With a brief mumbled farewell, she rushed to the carriage awaiting her beyond the gate.

Bennett turned at the click of heels on the marble floor. The ambassador stood in the hall behind him.

His cousin, Lord Henry Daller, studied the carriage. "Miss Sinclair has always been something of an odd duck, but I never imagined her showing up dressed like a native. You poor chap. You'll have your work cut out for you protecting her." He chuckled and pounded Bennett on the back. "I suppose it's to be expected, though, what with her background."

Bennett ground his teeth. Gossip. Yet another reason he preferred the battlefield to the drawing room. But even on the battlefield, it was essential to understand the terrain. So he smiled. "You sound as if you know a great deal about her."

Daller shrugged, a smooth, careless motion that Bennett didn't doubt had been carefully crafted to neither confirm nor deny. "It's my duty to know of His Majesty's citizens living in this land." He smoothed the thin chestnut mustache adorning his upper lip and paused.

Bennett forced out the question the ambassador obviously awaited. "So what can you tell me?"

The ambassador ushered Bennett toward his study, a slight, magnanimous smile sliding over his lips.

The heat in the study hung as oppressively as it had in the parlor. Bennett perched on the edge of the leather seat. He didn't make any more contact with the chair for fear of sticking to it when he tried to stand. He held out a slim hope that Daller would suggest they remove their jackets . . . but no, the man settled into his chair with apparent relish. Perhaps one grew accustomed to the heat?

Daller removed a silver snuffbox from his desk and gathered some onto his nail. He inhaled with a quick snort, then offered the box to Bennett.

Bennett refused with a shake of his head. *Get to the point.* Polite conversation had never been an art at which Bennett particularly excelled. He didn't see the point in wasting time with idle chatter. "What information do you have on Miss Sinclair?"

Daller steepled his fingers together. "Ah, our Miss Sinclair. Many of the local men are quite enchanted with her, although I believe that relates more to her friendship with Esad Pasha rather than any of her own . . . charms."

"Who is the pasha?"

"A former field marshal in the sultan's army. Now he serves as one of the sultan's advisers. They say he's trusted above all others."

Bennett filed that fact away. "Is the pasha friendly to the Crown?"

The ambassador frowned. "No more than the other locals. He swears complete allegiance to the sultan. But he does seem to have a genuine fondness for Miss Sinclair. He has acted as her father these past ten years."

Where was her real father? He hadn't escorted her today as Bennett had expected.

"Young men think to impress the pasha by composing inane poetry in her honor."

Bennett surreptitiously smoothed the front of his coat to ensure no bulge showed from the slim volume tucked within. He grimaced and lowered his hand. There was no need for that; no one knew about the poems he tried to write.

"There was actually quite a popular poem that made the rounds last year, comparing her hazel eyes to a mossy rock, of all things."

Every hair on Bennett's neck rose. "Hazel eyes?"

Daller nodded. "They are her most distinct feature. Such an odd collection of brown, green, and yellow. From her Greek mother, no doubt, all that mixed blood. Blood always shows."

The Miss Sinclair he'd met had brown eyes. Not even a half-blind swain would've called them hazel. Plain, chocolate brown. With so little else visible, he couldn't be mistaken.

"That woman wasn't Mari Sinclair."

So where was she? Had she been captured? Bennett tensed.

The ambassador stared. "Of course she was."

"That woman had brown eyes."

Daller stuttered in disbelief. "That was the Sinclair coach. I'm certain."

Bennett rose to his feet. If she'd been captured by the

Turks, he might already be too late. "I must locate Miss Sinclair."

Perhaps as a result of his diplomatic experience, the ambassador simply nodded at the sudden crisis. "We shall continue later."

Bennett strode from the room. He'd scouted the Sinclair residence after his arrival yesterday. The modest home was situated only a mile from the embassy. He'd ascertained on his short excursion that his horse provided little benefit on the narrow, crowded roads that connected them. He'd go on foot. He could be there by the time they saddled his horse.

The straight cobbled road in front of the embassy gave way to dirt roads that wove among the wood and stone buildings. Carriages and hand carts jostled for position in the narrow lanes, creeping and bumping in fits and starts as space became available. He hugged the left side of the street, claiming the meager shade offered by the top-heavy second stories of the houses, which extended a good four feet past the ground floor.

His heart hammered in his ears. He should've verified her safety last night rather than wasting time jotting down his impressions of Constantinople.

But he'd been unable to resist. Something about the city made his fingers itch to capture it with words.

He cut through a crowded marketplace. Greek, Turkish, and Persian voices shouted in good-natured banter intermixed with a collection of languages he couldn't even begin to decipher. A fortune's worth of curry and saffron spilled in pungent abundance from barrels and burlap sacks.

Men dressed in rich fabrics and those barely dressed at all intermingled freely in the space. Women cloaked in flowing rivers of cloth bought and sold beside the men, some with faces covered as the false Miss Sinclair's had been, but an equal number with faces bare.

He should have questioned the woman claiming to be Miss Sinclair about her use of the veil. He'd seen unveiled women yesterday. But he'd attributed her odd appearance to a woman too long in a strange land. Unforgivable. The mistake might have cost him his mission. And Miss Sinclair her life.

His boots crunched on the gritty road. Who was the unknown woman? If someone had harmed Miss Sinclair, why send a woman to take her place? It would, perhaps, buy them time until he realized his mistake. Time enough to torture Miss Sinclair until she confessed to espionage.

Or confess to anything they wanted just to stop the pain. Bennett's back burned in remembered agony. And the French were infants in torture compared to the Ottomans.

As he turned onto the block containing the Sinclair home, a carriage arrived. Bennett's eyes narrowed. That was the conveyance that had left the embassy a short time earlier. He gave brief thanks for the congested roads as he ducked behind a large date palm directly across the street.

The woman in bright gold emerged from the coach laughing. As she approached the house, the door opened and another female greeted her from the shadows of an arched entryway. The new woman wore a flowing blue robe similar to the false Miss Sinclair, but no veil hid the curls on her head. Her hair wasn't remarkable for its color, a rather nondescript brown, but for the sheer volume that tumbled down her back.

The woman in blue scanned the street.

Bennett tucked himself against the rough bark of the tree. Hers weren't the quick, darted glances his sisters used when they wished to avoid being caught in some prank, but rather the precise study of an experienced campaigner. Survey the land. Ensure no one tracked their movements.

After waiting a ten count, Bennett peered back around the tree as the woman finished her inspection and stepped into the sun. She issued an order in Turkish to the coachman. As she turned back to the house, sunlight illuminated her face, and for a moment, her eyes.

Hazel eyes.

Bennett's shoulders tensed. Ah, Miss Sinclair, it would seem. Free and unrestrained. Now that he'd seen her, there was no way he'd ever mistake her for the other woman. While they were about the same height, the other woman was built of generous curves, while Miss Sinclair displayed the lithe, subtle lines of a dancer.

The grace of one, too, apparently, as she darted into the house.

His fingers strayed to the book in his pocket, desperate to write. To transpose her essence onto paper.

Bennett started across the street, dashing the temptation from his thoughts. She was his assignment, not a bloody muse.

From now on, things would proceed according to his plans or not at all. She'd learn and learn quickly not to play such games with him. If she insisted on drawing, then she would damned well respect the dangers she'd brought on herself.

A thin, dark man slanted toward the house, his gait smooth and posture straight.

Bennett pulled back to his place behind the tree. One of the beaus the ambassador had mentioned? The door flew open at the stranger's approach, and Miss Sinclair raced toward him. Bennett braced for some tawdry lover's greeting. Instead, she stopped a few feet from the man. The Turkish man bowed, but she didn't return the gesture. A servant then.

Miss Sinclair draped a length of fabric over her hair and lower face as she talked. She nodded to the man once more, passed by him, and leaped into the carriage.

The coach jolted into motion.

What did she consider more important than a meeting to ensure her safety? Bennett swore under his breath and abandoned the scanty shade offered by the palm. She had agreed to work for the British army. It was time she learned to obey her commanding officer.

CHAPTER TWO

Mari choked on the cloyingly sweet smoke in the dark opium den. How could her father stand this place? She understood that once he'd smoked the opium, the room no doubt resembled a luxurious palace, but he chose to enter while still sober.

The lamps used to vaporize the noxious substance flickered dimly. She pushed aside the faded, filthy curtain enshrouding the bed the proprietor had pointed her toward. The man inside flinched at the sudden intrusion of light falling across his sallow complexion.

He offered her a beatific smile. "Mari-girl, how lovely to see you."

The tightness in her jaw made it near impossible to speak. "Time to come home, Father."

"Ah, but I'm having such a lovely time with all my friends here."

She glared at the odd assortment of men who littered the small establishment, all either in the process of losing themselves to opium or helping unfortunates to stay there.

"These men aren't your friends." She could have bitten her tongue as she spoke. She knew her arguments had no effect; why couldn't she stay her words?

"Ah, my dear, why are you upset? Am I late for tea, perhaps?"

She blinked back a stray tear. Confound the smoke. "Come."

He sat up in his small enclosure. She offered him a hand, but he waved it off. "Don't fret yourself." He swung his feet off the bench and rose, swaying dangerously. "It's a surprise that clarity of mind is not accompanied by clarity of motion." He chuckled at his wit.

Mari tucked herself under his arm before he fell. No, it wasn't a surprise. It had happened earlier this week and the week before and every week since she'd started fetching him home herself. She refused to meet the smirking gaze of the proprietor as she half dragged her father from the den. Luckily, her father had entered one of his languid moods and did nothing to resist her. He hummed tunelessly as they walked, lost in his own thoughts. She kept her head down to avoid the interested stares of the men drinking coffee outside at the nearby *kahve*. She hated to see the curiosity, or worse, pity in their eyes.

Only a few more seconds and they'd reach the coach. They would return home, and if the week was a good one, she'd be free from this for another four or five days. If it was a bad week . . . Well, she refused to think further on it.

A solid wall of green wool stepped into her path. Mari careened into it. Her father teetered in her hold until a large, scarred hand gripped her father's shoulder to steady him.

She grimaced and glared at the pale, puckered lines slashed across the back of the hand. She had to crane her neck to see more than the black braiding and silver buttons of his uniform. Feeling disadvantaged, she stepped back, dragging her father with her.

That hand did not match the rest of the man.

A tall, blond Adonis escaped from a Greek pedestal.

When Achilla, her maid, had described Mari's new protector in those terms earlier, Mari had attributed the effusive praise to her maid's approval of the male sex in general. After all, it hadn't taken much to convince Achilla to take her place at the meeting and get the first glimpse of Mari's protector.

Achilla hadn't exaggerated.

Mari shook off her initial awe. Ridiculous. His hand obviously belonged to him. She scanned him again. Indeed, his nose appeared as if it had been broken a time or two. His black eyelashes were definitely too long for a man and too dark for a man with golden hair. A small curved scar indented his left cheek, its color a shade lighter than the ruddy color staining his perfectly chiseled cheekbones.

Leave it to the British army to dress in a uniform designed for the damp dales of England while in an Ottoman summer. How exactly did he propose to ensure she did the Crown's bidding when he might expire from the heat at any moment? Her estimation of the man dipped further.

Confound it. She'd hoped by sending Achilla to the meeting this morning, she would be able to fetch her father without interference and buy herself a short respite.

She'd failed on both accounts.

His steel blue eyes raked her with an insultingly frank perusal. She stiffened. None of her servants would've betrayed her whereabouts. How had he found her?

Her arm tightened on her father. The major had followed her. Skulked after her like a common footpad. Her business here didn't involve him. It didn't concern the British government or affect the agreement to gather more information they'd coerced out of her. He had no right to intrude.

His eyes rested on her father, and pity entered into his gaze.

Her free hand clenched at her side. How dare he? How dare he judge her or her father? She stepped to the right to move around the major.

He mirrored her motion. "Miss Sinclair?"

Mari turned back the other way. He had followed her to the opium den, and he could trail her home because she had no intention of speaking to him here. Thanks to her father's weakness, her life provided enough fodder for public discourse. She refused to add to the subject matter.

The major blocked her again.

She exhaled through clenched teeth. "Would you be so good as to move, sir? My burden is not precisely light."

His eyes narrowed. "You're Miss Sinclair." The words were not a question.

Major Prestwood moved toward her father, but she led him a step out of the major's reach. "And you, sir, are arrogant and overbearing. Step aside."

He did not comply. "You could use my aid."

"I can manage. Besides, I don't know you."

His eyebrow rose. "If you had kept our appointment this morning, you would."

Mari glared at him, grateful her veil hid her blush. "As you can see, I had other pressing concerns."

"Concerns that should have been brought to me."

Mari had to count to ten before speaking. Insufferable, insufferable man. "I know nothing of you, sir, and from this brief acquaintance, I am convinced that I would be most pleased to keep it so. I did not ask for your assistance and I do not desire it."

Her words didn't have a noticeable effect on the man standing before her. In fact, he appeared bored by her outburst. "I'm to watch over you. My orders are clear whether you sanction them or not."

The man could teach a few things to a stone wall. Was he afraid she'd renege on her agreement? That she'd regain her senses and run away from all this? Her shoulder ached from supporting her father, and she shifted under the weight. Oh, she'd do their bidding. The British had ensured that.

And she'd been too weak to deny them.

She directed her disgust at him, grateful to have a target other than herself. "Fine. We will discuss it later over tea. Or do I have to clear that with you as well?"

Major Prestwood stiffened, and she gloried in provoking the small reaction.

"So much rage directed at the world," her father sighed next to her, startling her.

Mari gritted her teeth. Her father was right. There was no point in letting this man aggravate her. If she had her way, she wouldn't have to deal with him much longer.

As she calmed, however, she noted a low rumble. The men

at the *kahve* across the street gestured in her direction and argued with one another.

Oh heavens. It must appear a veiled woman was being accosted by a British soldier. Ottoman men took the safety of their women quite seriously.

Major Prestwood continued to glare at her. "Why do you wear this? You are British." He tugged on the corner of her veil, and it fell away from her face.

Two men at the *kahve* leaped to their feet with cries of outrage.

Her breath lodged in her throat and she darted them a quick glance.

Major Prestwood followed her gaze. The situation finally penetrated her protector's thick skull. His hand dropped to the hilt of his sword.

The aggressive action only further enraged their audience, and the two young, turbaned men pushed their chairs back with a clatter. Their yellow boots and clean-shaven faces marked them as Janissaries stationed in Constantinople, members of the sultan's overstaffed and underused military force. Men bored and longing for a fight. They drew their swords.

Mari bit back an oath. She had to save Major Prestwood. Although life would be much easier if she did not . . . She sighed and lowered her voice. "If you value your life and various parts of your anatomy, start walking with me to my coach."

She pulled her father, but he ignored her urgent tugs and kept strolling as if he hadn't a care. And considering his poppy-eaten state, he most likely didn't.

Staccato footsteps pounded on the road.

They wouldn't make it to the coach before the soldiers intercepted them.

Prestwood stepped closer to her side. "I'll hold them back while you get to safety."

Mari briefly closed her eyes. Perhaps she'd be doing the world a favor if she allowed the camel-headed man to be cut to pieces and left at the city gate. "I'm in no danger. They're advancing because they think you're accosting me."

Prestwood stepped back from her. "The devil you say."

"Just get in the coach. I'll deal with the men."

Prestwood glowered at her. "I will not leave you to face armed men."

The men were almost on top of them.

Confound it. Before she could rethink the monumental foolishness of her actions, she let go of her father and grabbed Major Prestwood by the front of his emerald jacket. "You are right, my love. We should never fight again!" She rose on tiptoe, and planted her lips on his hard, unyielding mouth.

The two Janissaries skidded to a halt mere feet from them, the steel of their swords glinting at the edge of her vision. They argued with each other in Turkish about the nature of the kiss.

She had to convince them. She pried Prestwood's hand from the hilt of his sword and then slowly slid her hands up the major's chest. Heavens, the man's lips weren't the only thing about him that was hard. She wrapped her arms around his neck, threading her fingers through the deceptively silken blond hair that escaped his hat to brush his collar. Sweet heavens, what good did it do for a man to have hair so soft?

The strands slid through her fingers, making her long to clench her hands tightly so they didn't escape her. Panting, she lifted her lips a scant inch from his. "Pull the veil from my hair so they can see who I am. I've been here to collect my father before."

Prestwood's arms wrapped around her waist and his lips softened, sweeping over hers. "If you are going to sell this as a lovers' quarrel, you need to act like you've been kissed before." He caught her gasp of outrage by deepening the kiss.

With a gentle tug, he drew the veil from her hair. He slowly sucked her bottom lip into his mouth, flicking his tongue over the trapped flesh.

But she wasn't about to let him control the kiss. This was her plan. And she had been kissed before, curse him. True, it had been absolutely nothing like this one, but if he was concerned about convincing their audience, he need not fear. She had read quite a bit on the subject.

She pressed herself more fully against him and copied what he'd just done to her lips. But her studies hadn't prepared her for the jolt of pleasure that came from the small hitch in his breathing. She wanted to crow in triumph, but then his hand dropped down to cup her backside—her backside!—and she was sure she'd be shocked later, but all she could think about now was trumping his move. And the fact that his body was pressing against all the spots begging to be touched, sending heat between her legs.

She groaned and shifted, her nipples rubbing the rough wool of his jacket though the silk of her caftan. She gasped at her audacity and the foreign sensation. Heavens, that was— she rubbed against him again—incredible.

What would his hands feel like there? Would his touch ease the burning or only increase it?

His hand caressed up her side, promising to reveal the answer. One more inch and his finger would brush the side of her breast. His hand stalled so close, the warmth of it heated the very flesh that ached for his touch.

Did he seek to drive her mad?

Wantonly, she leaned forward. But Prestwood stepped back, causing her to stumble.

The Janissaries had sheathed their swords. Around them, the crowd of men cheered and hooted.

How long ago had the danger passed? And how had she allowed herself to become so lost that she had no idea of the answer? She spun away and collected her father, who studied a rock in the road.

"Do you suppose this rock might have been trod upon by an ancient Roman?"

She helped him to his feet and resisted the urge to snap at him. "Perhaps, Father. Take it with you if you want." She turned back to check on Prestwood. He stood directly behind her. His face wore the same arrogant, bored expression from earlier.

The cad. As if she had not just saved his skin. As if he had not just kissed her so senseless she'd forgotten herself in the middle of a public square.

The British might have been able to blackmail her into continuing her work, but that didn't mean she had to accept the watchdog they sent to ensure she bowed to their wishes.

They might have been able to gain her compliance with threats, but they didn't control her as completely as they thought.

Bennett sat in the backward-facing seat of the coach and glared at the other two occupants. What in the blazes had just happened? Not only had he been so distracted by the aggravating Miss Sinclair that he'd failed to notice the discontented audience, but then he'd mauled her in the street like a randy recruit.

If he'd thought the urge to write about her strange, it was nothing compared to the yearning he now felt to touch her again. To experience the vibrancy that had shaken him to his core.

Experience the vibrancy?

Colonel Smollet-Green had been correct. Poetry led to weak, milksop officers.

Bennett had been too long on the battlefield and too long from the soft touch of a woman. Nothing more. He needed to bed one, not write about one.

He studied Miss Sinclair. Her hazel eyes were indeed incredible—soft brown pools stirred with ribbons of jade and flecks of gold surrounded by thick, dark lashes his sisters would have killed for. Her eyes slanted upward slightly at the corners, granting her an exotic, mysterious air that promised silken sheets, spiced oils, and nights of untold delight.

The eyes rested in a sun-kissed face underlined by strong cheekbones and a straight, Roman nose. Her lips—Bennett pulled his gaze from their seductive, just-kissed fullness. His memory was far too active to dwell on that feature.

Rather than a soft English kitten, she was a panther. And like a panther, she appeared ready to go for his throat.

He met the challenge in her gaze with one of his own. She shouldn't have tried to deceive him.

Completely and utterly unacceptable. Sophia had done that, allowing herself to be beaten time and time again.

Love for his sister had made him gullible and blind. He'd believed her when she had not attended family gatherings, claiming a sudden illness, even though she'd never been sickly as a child. He had believed her when she'd claimed the bruise on her cheek resulted from bumping into a door. Hell, he'd even teased her about it.

But he'd allow no emotions to interfere with his protection of Miss Sinclair. As soon as he received the locations the government wanted sketched, he'd arrange for her to draw them. Then he could leave.

Her hazel eyes flashed. "Stop glowering. It isn't my fault I had to save your life."

No, he wouldn't let her rouse him this time. "Thank you for your quick thinking."

She frowned and lowered her brows. Searching for the trap in his words, no doubt. She crossed her arms and stared out the window.

Her father, Sir Reginald, slouched next to her, a bemused smile on his face. Sir Reginald had given his daughter her coloring, but there the similarities ended. His face lacked the sharp angles that defined hers and his addiction had taken its toll, robbing the man's skin of luster and his eyes of life.

Miss Sinclair glanced at him and caught his survey of her father. She quickly turned back to glare at the pane of glass beside her. Too quickly.

He sought to put her at ease. "His sickness is no reflection on you."

Her mouth dropped open and her face jerked toward him.

"Of all the arrogant, overbearing— Why do you suppose for one minute that I care a whit for your opinion about me or my father? Just because some imbecile assigned me to you, it doesn't allow you free rein in my private life."

Bennett clenched the seat cushion until his fingers ached. Control. The army had taught him control. As a Rifleman, he could hide unmoving in the brush for hours while enemy troops moved inches from his position. A mere slip of a woman didn't have the power to rile him. "On the contrary, for the next month, it belongs to me entirely."

Hell, how had that escaped?

Miss Sinclair sputtered. "The devil it does!"

Bennett rubbed a hand over his eyes. "I'm here to protect you—"

"That's a polite way of putting it. I agreed to do the drawings, not to accept a jailer."

"You need to be alive to draw."

"How do you propose to accomplish that? Your very presence threatens to expose me. I risk discovery every day. The risk increases monumentally if I'm entangled with an obviously British keeper who knows nothing about the country he's been sent into."

Bennett's hands tightened on his knees. "What you are doing for the British is dangerous. Your ridiculous scenes put your life in jeopardy. Who did I meet with this morning?"

Staring at him defiantly, she folded the veil with crisp, tight snaps. "My maid."

Without the guidance of her father, she'd grown too wild. Her excessive freedom ended here. "What are your plans for the rest of the afternoon?"

Her lips stretched over her teeth in an expression that was more snarl than smile. "I'm busy."

"With what?"

She lifted her chin and shrugged. "It doesn't concern my work so it doesn't concern you."

"Your plans?" He waited silently, never letting his attention waver from her, a trick that had wrung information from the most hardened soldiers.

Apparently, Miss Sinclair was made of sterner stuff. When they drew to a halt at her residence, she still hadn't answered him.

He jumped down, then assisted her out. The touch of her skin was as disturbing as before.

As if he were Prometheus holding stolen fire.

When she tried to pull away, he refused to let her, locking his fingers around her wrist. Her pulse fluttered under his fingers.

"Unhand me."

"Not until I know what you are planning." And until he convinced his brain that there was nothing extraordinary about this woman except her foolishness.

Suddenly, she twisted in his grasp, freeing herself. But he grabbed her waist before she'd managed a single step. The lithe muscles under his fingers tensed, and he tightened his hold before her next attempt to flee. "If you don't tell me your plans, we will stand here all night."

She shoved against his chest with both hands, but when that didn't loosen his hold, she sighed. "I'll stay at my house tonight like an obedient puppy."

Bennett nodded at the concession. Good, perhaps she

could learn who was in charge after all. "We'll discuss my plans for you tomorrow morning at nine."

She nodded.

"Do I have your word that you'll not try to leave the house this evening?"

She glared at him. "If it convinces you to let go of me, then yes, you have my word."

He loosened his grip, and she stalked away toward the coach.

Despite her glares and muttered oaths, he helped her remove her father. Once the man's feet were on the ground, he teetered for a moment, then straightened and practically skipped into the house. She stalked after him, the silk of her robe clinging to softly supple hips.

She'd never agree to confine her movements to a carefully arranged schedule. Even knowing what little he did of her, his original stratagem was ridiculous. So rather than monitoring her from afar he'd have to—

Damnation. He wouldn't be able to leave her side.

An Excerpt from
SINS OF A VIRGIN

PROLOGUE

Three glasses of the finest French brandy lingered untouched on the desk. Sir James Glavenstroke tapped his own half-empty glass with nervous fingers. He never should have poured the drinks before they entered the room. That had guaranteed they wouldn't imbibe. Which was a damned shame. Alcohol would have made the upcoming ordeal easier.

At least for him.

The Trio, they called themselves—La Petit, Cipher, and Wraith. The finest agents he'd ever created. More soldiers owed their lives to them than to Wellington himself.

Pride burned in Glavenstroke's chest, but he coughed it away. After all, any one of them would gladly slit his throat for the hell he'd damned them into.

Not that they'd be any happier when he kicked them out of it.

Glavenstroke ran a hand through his thinning gray hair, then sipped his brandy. Madeline Valdan, La Petit, watched his fidgeting with far too keen a gaze. The past ten years had transformed Madeline from a breathtaking youth to the most achingly beautiful woman he'd ever seen. He tried to still his nervous motions, but he knew that, in and of itself, would be a sign.

"What are you stewing over, Glavenstroke?" Madeline asked. "You know you can't hide anything from us."

No. He'd been unable to do that since he plucked them from their fate on the gallows. In exchange for their lives, they'd agreed to hone their particular skills on behalf of His Majesty's government. They'd each originally possessed talents that had led him to select them over the other condemned souls in Newgate, but once they'd received formal training, they'd become an unstoppable force. A wickedly sharp dagger used to eviscerate Napoleon and his allies.

But now the war was over.

"Out with it." As always, the voice of the Cipher, Clayton Campbell, remained perfectly calm, yet drew a shiver up Glavenstroke's spine.

With a sigh, he removed the bank drafts from the drawer and laid them on the oak desk. "The Foreign Office thanks you for your hard years of service on His Majesty's behalf."

"But?" prompted Madeline.

"There is no *but*. You've served your country well and are free to resume normal lives. You each have, of course, received full pardons for your past transgressions."

Madeline and Clayton stared at him. It was a measure of their level of shock that they permitted that much of a reaction.

Ian Maddox, the Wraith and third member of the Trio, was the only one who remained unsurprised. But Glavenstroke knew that stemmed from his low expectations of humanity in general. Unlike the other two, Ian was a product of the mean streets in London's West End. No level of cruelty or greed surprised him. The government could have ordered their immediate execution and he wouldn't have batted an eye.

Madeline tucked a strand of chestnut hair behind her ear—the one nervous gesture he'd never been able to break her of. "Why?"

Ian's powerful frame relaxed in the chair, and rather than diminishing his strength, the pose made him resemble a tiger the moment before it pounced. "What dear Glaves here is too polite to say is that they don't need us anymore. Now that we're of no use to them, having us on the payroll is too much of a risk. Can't afford to let the sweetly docile populace discover they're employing the hangman's leftovers."

Ian was correct as always. In fact, with his ability to gain access to whatever location he desired, it was likely he'd known about this forced retirement before Glavenstroke did.

With an uncomfortable cough, Glavenstroke delivered the final insult—the bank drafts.

"This is the first pension payment?" Clayton's hand tensed on the slip of paper.

Ian snorted. "Sorry, they can't have us on the pension records, either."

Madeline stiffened. "I've whored myself on behalf of this country. A foot soldier would have made more than this."

Glavenstroke took a large swig of his brandy, welcoming the muted burn at the back of his throat. He'd called in every favor owed him to arrange for even this much. But he hadn't reached his current position by being soft, so he didn't apologize. After all, without his help, the three of them would've been dead a decade ago.

Clayton rested his hand on Madeline's arm. "With proper investment—"

"And what, another ten or twenty years of waiting? I know you're a genius with numbers, Clayton, but even you cannot miraculously transform this into anything other than the insult it is." She rose to her feet, and the other two followed.

"What do you plan to do?" Glavenstroke asked them, despising himself for the weakness the question betrayed.

Ian glanced back over his shoulder, a slight smile quirking the corner of his mouth. "Won't that thought keep you up at night?"

As the door closed silently behind them, Glavenstroke poured himself another glass of the amber liquid. They'd land on their feet. He'd taught them well.

Hopefully, they'd continue to use their skills to help society, because if any one of them turned—he knocked back the second shot of brandy in a single gulp—heaven help Mother England.

CHAPTER ONE

When lightning didn't strike Madeline Valdan as she strolled through the hallowed doors of White's, a wicked smile curved her lips. She'd seize her positive omens where she could.

While the footman by the door kept his gaze studiously averted, she slipped the heavy bag of gold sovereigns into his pocket and then rose up on tiptoe so her lips brushed the air inches from his ear. "Thank you, John." He still didn't deign to speak to her, but an adorable blush spread above the starched points of his shirt collar.

As she sauntered down the corridor, Madeline couldn't resist a quick gawk at this bastion of manliness. Marble pillars jutted out from deep, plush carpet to join with the ornate plaster of the ceiling and reflect the rippling patterns cast by the crystal chandeliers. The club reeked of power and entitlement.

And most importantly, money.

Madeline smoothed the flowing lines of her black domino. The silk used to make the cloak had been an extravagant expense, but as she'd learned, presentation was everything.

She strode past the coffee room and straight into the card room. After all, she was offering a gamble—hopefully, a very expensive gamble.

The murmur of masculine voices rumbled through the expansive space, punctuated by an occasional bark of laughter. Faro cards slapped onto tables and dice clacked across tables.

She scanned the room as she'd been trained, noting the number of men and classifying them: those actively gambling, those pretending to gamble, and those watching; those holding a winning hand versus a losing hand. From her brief glance, she also knew which men were dangerous and which posed a threat only to their after-supper pudding.

As Madeline walked to the center of the room, the tables she passed quieted, then burst into jumbled exclamations.

She selected a table directly in the center of the room under an immense glittering chandelier. She couldn't have asked for a better stage.

She smiled at the nervous young man who had turned to gape at her as she approached. She held out her hand. "Be a dear, Algie?"

Algie's training as a gentleman didn't fail her, and he offered his hand without thinking. She grasped it, stepped on his thigh, and then onto the middle of the table.

Madeline now held the attention of the entire group of assembled men.

Two determined footmen arrived at the edge of the table. "Miss, this isn't that type of establishment. You must leave or we will remove you."

Madeline threw back the hood of her cloak.

"Madeline . . ."

"Who's mistress . . ."

". . . seen with the Regent himself last . . ."

The voices testified that the last six months had served their purpose. They all knew who she was.

She'd spent every last dime of the paltry government stipend on being seen and heard around London. Dressed to scandalous perfection. Always on the arm of a different man and always on the cusp of something utterly outrageous. Soon the gossip sheets hadn't been able to write enough about her. Gentlemen lusted after her and ladies despised her.

She opened the front of her domino, revealing her emerald gown. The bodice skimmed her breasts and barely covered her nipples. In fact, when she'd tried it on, a misplaced sneeze had produced quite shocking results. The sleeves were practically nonexistent, and the lack of petticoats molded the skirt to every curve of her hip and leg.

She raised her voice to carry above the noise. "What do you think, gentlemen, shall I leave, or do you want to hear what inspired this dastardly stunt?"

The shouts clamoring for her answer overwhelmed the cries for her ousting, so the flustered servants stepped back a pace.

Madeline trailed a hand slowly down her hip. "I bring you something for sale." She nodded at offers shouted by several of the bolder gentlemen to share their beds for the night. "Not quite. I'm here to inform you of an auction."

"What's being sold?" asked the overdressed and overfed Colonel Willington.

She scanned the room, gauging the reactions. Excellent.

Every single one of them strained for her answer. She waited three more heartbeats before answering. "My virginity."

Disbelief and outrage echoed through the room. Forgotten cards drifted onto tables as fortunes sat neglected in the center. She didn't even try to speak for several minutes. But when she did, everyone listened. "The bidding book will be at Naughton's for the next fortnight." Most of the men here knew of the gambling den firsthand, and those who didn't wouldn't be bidding regardless. "At the end of those two weeks, the man with the highest bid wins."

"What exactly does he win?" a dark-haired fellow asked.

She tapped her cheek. "Hmm . . . my virginity?"

The crowd laughed, but he pressed on. "But what exactly does that entail?"

"That's simple. One night with me and a chance to succeed where every other man in London has failed."

A voice that she couldn't quite match with a face spoke from the corner of the room. "If you're a virgin, why not marry?"

She'd rather be dragged over broken glass by a herd of gout-ridden turtles. Yet she allowed none of her thoughts to show on her face when she lifted her eyebrow. "Is that an offer?" As she waited for the chuckles to die down, she untied her cloak, dropping it so it pooled at her feet. Eyes once again riveted to the ample amount of bosom she'd arranged for display. "I think you gentlemen know—mistresses have more fun."

Murmurs swelled again through the crowd until Baron Weltyn, a perspiring gentleman with a salmon-colored jacket and slightly bulging eyes, snorted. "But why would we want to bed an innocent?"

"While I may be a virgin . . ." She reached up and unbuckled the specially designed clasps on the shoulders of the gown. With a slight shrug, the dress joined the cloak on the ground, revealing her tightly laced black corset, matching satin drawers, and sheer stockings. "I'm definitely no innocent."

Men jumped to their feet, some driven by outrage, some by lust. Friends pounded the elderly Duke of Avelsy on the back as he choked on his brandy.

She surveyed the uproar with satisfaction. The only bad reaction was no reaction at all. For this auction to succeed, the scandal needed to sweep London. The more this night grew in infamy, the better she would do. Madeline reached up and plucked the pins from her hair so the dark chestnut strands tumbled over her shoulders and cascaded down her back.

The room again quieted.

Desire pounded hot and almost palpable in the room.

"How do we know you're a virgin?"

Finally, someone had the nerve to ask the question she'd seen burning in everyone's eyes. She peered into the darkened corners of the room. Ah, the not-so-honorable George Glinton.

"You've been escorted around London by nearly every peer in this room. How do we know you're still a virgin?"

"Can any of you claim to have bedded me?" She reached leisurely to her feet and retrieved her dress and domino, treating the men in front of her to the view of her breasts threatening to overflow the cups of her corset, while the men behind her watched the fabric of her drawers tightening over her backside. Satisfied that she had their full attention, she draped her clothing over her arm and held out her hand so

Algie could assist her to the ground. With swaying hips, she walked toward the door.

"Wait!" another voice shouted. "You didn't answer Glinton. How do we know you're a virgin?"

She peered back over her shoulder and smiled that seductive smile she'd been forced to perfect during countless hours of training by the Foreign Office. "It is a gamble, is it not? And that, gentlemen, is why you will have to bid and bid well."

Chapter Two

Gabriel Huntford kept his arms folded so he didn't beat some sense into the man. "Of course it's the same murderer."

Jeremiah Potts, magistrate of the Bow Street Office, mopped his perpetually damp brow with a square of linen. "Girls are strangled in London all the time."

"My sister's body was arranged exactly the same."

"In a nightgown in a bed. Half the blasted corpses we find have been murdered in their beds." Potts sat heavily behind his desk. "Why would the murderer have waited so long to kill again? It makes no sense. Your sister's case was put aside seven years ago."

Only in the official records. Not a day had passed when Gabriel hadn't searched for some clue he might have missed. Or for the mysterious gentleman his twin had mentioned before her death. Now he finally had suspects. Solid leads. Unfortunately, they resulted from another dead girl. "I'm the best Runner you've got."

Potts sighed, the lines creasing his forehead suddenly more pronounced. "Not for this case. If it's related to your sister's—and I'm not saying I agree with you on that—you're too close."

"You hired me because of my work on my sister's case."

"It was either that or arrest you for disturbing the public peace." Potts continued, "It took me over a year to smooth the feathers you ruffled. I'm not going to let you run roughshod through the richest, most powerful men in England based on the word of a half-blind, pensioned-off coachman who spends his days drunk in a tavern."

"A tavern directly across from the school where the dead woman taught. The man does nothing but sit and watch people come and go. He's a witness. He saw Miss Simm meet a gentleman and leave in his coach."

"A rented hackney."

"But the gentleman in the hackney had visited to the school before."

"In a coach with a coat of arms containing some sort of animal. I know. I read your report. I also read that your witness had no physical description of the man other than that he was tall, well-dressed, and blurry. You will not accuse innocent men on such unreliable evidence."

"In other words, you'd rather let a killer go free than risk questioning the aristocracy."

"Those gentlemen are the ones who assign us a budget every year. You may not like it, but if they cut our budget again, we'll lose two more Runners. Do you realize how many more criminals will remain on the streets if that happens? Besides, the Simm murder will be investigated. Just not by you."

Gabriel reminded himself that he respected Potts on most days. And he didn't envy him the groveling he performed to keep Parliament happy. But in this he was wrong. No one knew the details of this case or his sister's as he did. He was the one who had interviewed the witnesses from both murders. He was the one who'd recorded every detail from the scene of the crimes. He couldn't risk someone else not being as thorough. Or risk them not pressing hard enough because they were afraid to offend the high-and-mighty aristocracy. "I'll investigate on my own."

He'd finally been given what he'd searched for these past years. Suspects. After his sister's murder, the only thing he knew was that she'd been seen with a mysterious gentleman. But now with this new murder, he'd been able to cross-check his list of the noblemen who'd been in London at the time of his sister's murder with a list of men who had daughters at the school. And since the school, for the most part, housed bastard daughters of rich aristocrats, the list was quite small. When he'd further tightened the list to those with animals on their family crests, he'd been left with a list of seven names.

"Do you think your suspects will talk to you without the authority of Bow Street behind you? They won't even let you in the door. And if you go against my word on this, you'll no longer be . . ." Potts stared at something outside his office door, his mouth gaping.

Gabriel turned, curious as to what had rendered Potts speechless in the middle of one of his prized threats. The only time he could recall Potts at a loss for words was when that albino man and his camel—

Gabriel's breath escaped as if he'd been punched in the gut.

A woman stood in the doorway.

No. That would be like calling the Holy Grail a drinking cup.

If his every dark, midnight fantasy had somehow come to life, they would have created this woman. And since she'd been drawn from his dreams, he already knew the rich, dark curls artfully arranged on her head would be silky to his touch. He knew when she turned, a few lucky tendrils would have escaped to tease the slender column of her throat. He recognized the pert, straight nose, ached to run his finger over the delicate curve of her ear.

But it was her lips he couldn't look away from. Lips his imagination never could have conjured. Lush, sensuous, and dark, as if she'd just sipped a glass of fine red wine. He wanted to bring his mouth to hers, sample her flavor, and grow drunk on her sweetness.

A slight mocking curve of that mouth brought his attention to her eyes. After his intense study, it was a bit of a shock to find she wasn't looking at him at all, but rather over his shoulder at Potts.

She stepped into the room, the small, graceful movement drawing Gabriel's attention to her body. Her gown was no different from ones he saw every day in Hyde Park, yet it was infinitely more provocative. The bodice offered up the lush perfection of her breasts. The narrow skirt highlighted the tiny span of her waist and gentle flare of her hips.

"Mr. Potts, I can wait if you need more time," the woman said, her voice the perfect mixture of sugar and seduction.

Potts lumbered out from behind his desk and caught the woman's hand, bringing it to his lips as ruddy color darkened his cheeks. "No, Miss Valdan. I let time get away from me. We were finished."

The name doused Gabriel's lustful appreciation. Madeline Valdan. The courtesan's name had been on every male's lips for the past six months. Yesterday, with the start of her ridiculous auction, it had grown ten times worse. Hell, at the murder scene yesterday, the other constables had been unable to focus on anything save their lamentable lack of funds for bidding on her.

Potts led Miss Valdan to the worn leather chair across from his desk and motioned for her to sit, then turned to Gabriel. "Huntford, the matter is decided. You have other cases. Other people who deserve justice."

When Potts said his name, Miss Valdan finally directed her gaze to him. It swept over him like velvet, leaving his skin hot and itchy. But Gabriel resisted the urge to straighten like a green youth; instead, he met her eyes with a glare. He had a murder to solve—a murder he would solve quickly if Potts would just see reason. But he now had to waste precious time as Potts fawned over London's favorite courtesan, forgetting he was old enough to be her father.

"That will be all, Huntford."

Potts might tolerate Gabriel's arguments in private, but Gabriel knew better than to question the man in public. "Yes, sir."

Miss Valdan watched them with amused tolerance, somehow making the cracked leather chair look soft and comfortable, as if she'd climbed onto the lap of a lover.

He had better things to do than provide amusement. Gabriel strode from the room, glad to be out of the stilted air of Potts's office so he could pull oxygen more easily into his lungs.

Potts quickly shut the door behind him.

Chaos erupted as the criminals and constables alike regained their senses now that Miss Valdan was no longer in sight. The shouting started. The crying. The gruff orders.

Gabriel ignored them, locked his arms over his chest, and waited. What could she need? Help finding some bauble she'd misplaced? He had a murder to solve. Despite Potts's denial, there was no doubt that it was the same murderer. Both women had been strangled and their bodies arranged in a cheap rented room. They had both been dressed in a white nightgown with a mourning brooch pinned at their throats. Gabriel fingered the brooch in his pocket, the one that had been pinned to his sister. It held a lock of her hair sealed under glass. The one pinned to Miss Simm had held a piece of hers. The brooch was a taunt by the murderer to show he'd known his victims in advance—known them well enough to get a lock of hair. Every day Gabriel was tempted to crush the damned thing beneath his heel. But he couldn't. It was a clue, one of the only ones he had.

The door suddenly opened, and Miss Valdan appeared. "I shall expect him at eleven tomorrow."

Potts bowed deeply from his place near the door. "It's our pleasure, Madeline."

Gabriel held his ground outside the doorway so Potts wouldn't be able to avoid him. Miss Valdan would have to step around him to exit, but she could survive the slight inconvenience. Everyone else might bow to her whims, but Gabriel had more important priorities.

Yet rather than skirting around, Miss Valdan sauntered straight forward as if he weren't there. For a second, Gabriel feared she might careen into him, but despite the possible collision, he wouldn't scamper out of her way. She could damned well alter her course.

She didn't.

Her chosen path brushed so close to him that her dress caressed his leg and the hint of vanilla in her hair teased his nostrils.

A small smile lifted her lips. "I'll see you soon."

She had to have been talking to Potts. Yet dread settled in Gabriel's gut.

Potts cleared his throat. "You have a new assignment, Huntford."

M adeline handed the heavy bouquet of scarlet orchids to the wan-faced girl who waited at the kitchen entrance.

The girl's eyes widened as she tucked the blossoms into her basket. "Lawks, miss. I doubt any of the fellows on the street will be able to afford this."

Madeline tried not to notice the threadbare patches on the girl's shawl. After paying her butler and coachman for the two remaining weeks of the auction, and her trip to Bow Street, she was about equally poor. Besides, advice was worth far more than her few remaining farthings. "You have two options. Either break it down into smaller bouquets or sell it to one of the flower shops. These are from the Duke of Umberland's private hothouse. They're the only ones of their kind in England. Don't take less than a guinea for the bunch of them."

"Thank you, miss." Tears glistened in the girl's brown eyes.

Madeline stepped back. Why did they always complicate things by becoming emotional? "Just make sure you don't spend the money on trinkets. Use it to buy more flowers."

The girl nodded, holding the basket to her chest. "Think you'll have more flowers for us girls tomorrow, miss?"

"Undoubtedly." Did the men of London think she wanted to drown in them? "Oh, and there's a forbidding man standing at my front door. Can you leave without him seeing you?"

The child's head bobbed. "I'm good at that."

Madeline shut the door, aware of her butler hovering behind her. "Orchids make me sneeze," she explained.

"And the roses, and the daffodils, and the peonies? I must say your sneezing was becoming bothersome."

"Terrible curse." Madeline crossed her arms and silently dared him to contradict her.

"Indeed, miss."

Madeline eyed her butler, her eyes rising to the top of his head. "The feather does look better on you."

Canterbury patted the ostrich feather on his hat. "Indeed, miss." The jaunty trimming she'd given him fluttered over his high-crowned beaver, a new addition in his seemingly endless supply of unusual creations. "Thank you."

She still wasn't sure how her butler knew Wraith. Neither of them would speak about it. All she knew was that

Wraith had hired him for her because he was trustworthy. And Wraith didn't think anyone was trustworthy. "Well, as you said, it never suited my lavender bonnet."

Canterbury glanced toward the doorway. "Shall I answer the door now, miss?"

Madeline walked in the opposite direction. "Give him another minute, then put him in the study."

"Shall I tell him you will attend him shortly?"

"No. Our appointment isn't for another half an hour." She had no problem making the Runner wait until then. She was hiring him, not the other way around. If he was going to prove impossible to work with, she needed to know immediately.

"Very good, miss."

Madeline hurried up the stairs to the parlor. The room provided a clear view of the front door where Huntford waited.

As before, a tingle slid down her spine. It was a primal response, one she'd experienced only when her life was in danger. She shouldn't be in danger now, yet her senses sharpened. The clatter of each horse hoof. The glint of the sun on the puddle behind him. She became aware of the weight of the knife sheathed at her calf.

Even though Huntford's second knock had gone unanswered for several minutes, he still waited on her doorstep. He didn't fidget. He hadn't turned away in frustration. He simply waited. Still and silent like a wolf.

An arrogant wolf.

Below, the door opened. Huntford must have been surprised by her butler's hat—she often had to fight the urge to blink owlishly at him herself—but the Runner's posture didn't change. He simply removed his own hat and stepped inside.

Madeline moved to the door that joined the parlor to the study. Cracking the door open, she waited as the footsteps sounded on the stairs.

A moment later, Canterbury ushered Huntford inside. "Miss Valdan will see you when she is available."

Huntford nodded once. When the door closed silently behind Canterbury, Huntford remained in place while his eyes searched the room. She didn't doubt he saw everything from the ink stain on the desk to the threadbare patch on the rug, and he never once allowed his back to be to the door.

Perhaps he might be of some use after all.

She also liked the way he stood, weight centered, arms loose. There were scabs on his knuckles, too—at most, a week old. The calluses on his hands were far older.

His clothing gave her pause, however. Ian had said he'd earned a fair amount of money from his private investigations, but she wouldn't have picked him as a man to spend much of it on clothing. But there was no doubt that his clothing wasn't some ready-made attire. It had been tailored specifically for him, skimming his broad shoulders and trim waist. The cravat at his neck was tied simply, but with crisp, clean lines. His boots, while not new, were polished to a shine.

Who was he trying to prove himself to?

Not her. He'd been dressed just as precisely at the police office yesterday.

Huntford's gaze swung to the door she was hiding behind. He couldn't see her. She knew that. She'd hidden this way a hundred times before. She was out of sight. Her breathing was light and shallow through her nose. There were no shadows under the door. There was no way he could know she was there.

Yet when his attention lingered there, she had to fight the urge to back away, her heart fluttering in her chest like that of a cornered rabbit.

Madeline narrowed her gaze, annoyed at her body's betrayal.

Huntford suddenly disappeared from sight and Madeline had to shift to find him again. He stood at her desk, flipping through the blank sheets of paper on top. After a quick pause, he moved behind it and opened a drawer. When he discovered that the only thing inside was a list of her current bidders, he'd be disappointed.

Madeline smiled. She'd intended to make him wait until eleven but this was too good an opportunity to pass up. Keeping her steps silent, she left the parlor and walked to the study door.

Gabriel's hand rested on the brass drawer handle. He'd meant to come here and refuse the assignment, a task Potts thought so important that he'd reassigned not only the Simm murder, but all Gabriel's other cases until Miss Valdan's job was complete. But now Gabriel stared at the page of names. It must be a list of the men bidding on her.

Lenton. Billingsgate. Darby. The names seared across his mind. They were three of his suspects.

Potts had said she wanted to hire a Runner to investigate the men bidding on her. What if he could use her investigation to hide his own? Potts was right, most of his suspects would do everything they could to avoid a murder investigation. But if they meant to win Miss Valdan, they'd be willing to—

The door suddenly swung open.

Miss Valdan paused in the doorway, eyebrow raised, her gaze on the paper in his hand. Gabriel straightened but he didn't bother to scramble away from the open drawer. It was too late for that. But why hadn't he heard her coming? And damnation, his cheeks were heating like he was an errant child.

She inclined her head. "Can I help you locate something?"

Gabriel shrugged. "I thought since you were occupied, I'd leave a note and come back when you were available."

She glanced pointedly at the blank paper and ink on the top of the desk. She didn't believe him, but then he hadn't really expected her to.

"Like at eleven, our appointment time?"

"I'm afraid I have a pressing matter to attend to then." Because he hadn't thought he'd stay here longer than it took to refuse her job.

Madeline checked the clock on the mantel, then gestured to the door with a flick of her hand. "Well, it's almost eleven now. If you cannot stay, feel free to send someone in your place."

Gabriel almost agreed. But those three names on the list beckoned, too tempting to ignore.

No, he needed to stay even if it meant giving her the capitulation she sought. "The other meeting can be postponed." Hopefully. His witness, the old coachman, Bourne, was always at the tavern. Gabriel could ask his additional questions later.

"Good. I assume Potts told you what I will require?"

"He did, but perhaps you should tell me so there will be no misunderstandings."

She walked toward him. Gabriel moved to the other side of the desk, reluctant to have her near him again. Rather than claim the chair as he'd expected, she stopped and glanced out the window.

The daylight poured across her face, and Gabriel studied her afresh. Surely the unforgiving rays of the sun would reveal some flaw. A freckle. A pockmark. A heavy dusting of rice powder. But if anything, the sun rendered her skin more radiant. More pristine.

His teeth ground together as lust rose unbidden. Everything from the lush cupid's bow of her lips to the way her fingers rubbed at a knot in her lower back whispered of sensuality. It surrounded her like fine perfume. It wasn't gaudy or overpowering, but rather a subtle fragrance that drew one closer to explore the complex notes.

Her eyes lifted from the window, sweeping him with similar methodical intensity. And being male, part of him was very curious what she concluded.

Hell. He didn't want Miss Valdan. He wanted to catch a murderer. "What is it you require?" he asked, his voice curt even to his own ears.

She shrugged, drawing his eyes to the luscious hint of bosom visible above the neckline of her cream-colored dress. "Contrary to what you obviously believe, Mr. Huntford, I'm not a fool. I need to be sure of two things—first and foremost, that the man who wins can pay. I need you to examine the bidders' financial records and discover if they have the blunt to honor their bids." She sat and straightened the papers on her desk. "I'm not going to hand over my virginity on the empty promise of being paid in the future. I want my money as soon as the deed is done."

Gabriel looked for any sign that she wasn't as cold about the pronouncement as she appeared. But she met his gaze without flinching. He further resolved to ignore his baser urges. A woman who could sell her virginity without any hesitance must have ice in her veins.

Or wasn't truly a virgin.

Yet that suspicion didn't matter if she gained him access to what he needed. If he had his suspects' financial records, there was a chance he'd be able to find some tie to both murders. The purchase of the mourning brooches, perhaps?

Yet in his experience, gentlemen weren't eager to part with anything, let alone their most private financial dealings. "What makes you think anyone will comply with your demand for proof?"

"Because I'll ask them."

Curse it. Perhaps it would be best to refuse the assignment after all. If that was her plan, she had about as much chance of succeeding as he did on his own. "And if they don't agree, Miss Valdan?"

The steady calm in her gaze fractured and she rose to her feet. She chewed nervously on her lip, leaving it moist and rosy. "Madeline. My name is Madeline." She peered up at him with wide eyes. "They will agree, won't they? I mean, it makes sense." She placed her hand on his chest, its weight light, uncertain. "I didn't want to do this, but what other option do I have? What lady would trust me in her house as a maid? And I'm not well-bred enough to be a governess."

Despite the seductive warmth of her touch, he wasn't about to feel sorry for her. He removed her hand. "You chose this."

She drew in a deep breath. "You're right. And I do have a plan."

"Your plan is to *ask* them?"

"It's a good plan. The men are gentlemen. They'll honor their bets." When her hands trembled, she tucked them behind her.

Heaven save him from naive fools. Without her veneer of bravado, she appeared barely out of the schoolroom. "Just because they're gentlemen doesn't mean they'll act like it." He wanted to brush his thumb across her lower lip to save it from the abuse of her teeth, but he feared if he touched her lips, he'd want to touch the slender column of her throat. And once his fingers had skimmed over her throat, he'd be unable to stop them from dipping lower.

And he wasn't one of her lovesick swains.

"You'll help me?" She reached for him again but then dropped her hand as if afraid of rejection.

The small sign of vulnerability ensnared him in a way her seductive glances never could. "I'll do what I can."

Her breath came fast and shallow, causing her breasts to strain against her bodice. "I know."

He swallowed roughly as she leaned toward him. He needed to tell her he wasn't interested. But when he spoke, his voice was raspy and deep. "Madeline—"

She pulled back with quick determination. "That is why they'll agree."

He stared at her through the muddled haze of lust. "What?"

She dusted off the front of her gown as if to rid it of any hint of their interaction. "Every man has a weakness. Pride, vanity . . ." She allowed a deliberate pause, a mocking grin curving her lips. "The desire to protect. Any weakness can be turned to my advantage."

Gabriel stalked to the far corner of the room until the urge to wrap his hands around her neck faded. She had played him. She hadn't even needed to snap her fingers to bring him to heel. "You intend to manipulate every man in England?"

"As amusing as that would be, it isn't necessary. Once the first few agree, I'll point out that anyone who refuses must have something embarrassing to hide."

He exhaled through clenched teeth. *Forget she made a fool of you.* He'd wanted her to have a plan, and apparently, hers was far better than he'd given her credit for. But fury, and a disturbing amount of frustrated desire, still drove him. "So you plan to dupe them into paying you a fortune?"

She frowned. "No. They'll get what they pay for. My virginity. I'm merely trying to ensure they don't cheat me."

"By preying on their weaknesses."

She crossed her arms. "It's not a crime to discover fantasies. You do the same thing."

He glared at her. "Nonsense."

"When you capture a suspect, you ferret out their weaknesses first, do you not? You watch for the lies and the fears, then you exploit them to gain a confession. The only difference is that my process ends with a pleasant interlude in bed and yours ends on the gallows."

His fists tightened until his hands ached. But Miss Valdan was right, curse her. Besides, he couldn't risk provoking her further. The more he thought about it, the more perfect this opportunity was. By working for Madeline, he could investigate the men of the *ton* without their knowledge. Hell, perhaps they'd even help. "What else do you need me to do?"

She hesitated, and for a moment, he was positive his bitterness had lost him the assignment.

The door opened and the butler entered. This time a blue ribbon and pheasant feathers trimmed the man's hat. He carried a tray containing tea and biscuits, which he set on a small table. Madeline didn't spare the butler's strange attire a second glance. Instead, she lowered herself onto the settee and motioned to the chair across from her.

Gabriel sat. He'd be harder to throw out if he was drinking tea.

She poured with a grace more befitting a lady of the manor than a woman of the streets. Even his mother would have approved. She offered him a plate of biscuits. "I will also require the sexual histories of the top bidders. That information, I assume, they will be less anxious to part with."

At least she'd decided not to throw him out.

"My desire to fulfill fantasies only goes so far. I won't share a bed with a madman, no matter how much he pays. Nor do I want to end up with the pox as a memento of the evening. While financial information can be supplied by a banker or solicitor, this portion of the assignment will require an investigator familiar with the darker environs and back alleys of London."

That he was. Since Susan's death, he'd spent little time anywhere else. The more violent and depraved the criminal he hunted, the better. He held out hope with each arrest that someone would have a clue that would lead him to his sister's killer. As the months and years had passed, he'd recognized the growing improbability of that hope. Yet he couldn't stop.

Besides, if Miss Valdan wanted a proper investigation, not only would he look into the whorehouses and bordellos, he'd have to interview her bidders' staffs as well—butlers, valets, maids. All people who would know of their masters' proclivities.

And their whereabouts the night of the Simm murder.

Gabriel nodded in acceptance.

"Also, for the next fortnight, I need you by my side when I'm seen in public."

"What?" That sneaky cur Potts had left out that detail. "I can't investigate if I'm escorting you."

"I'm not asking for much time. A couple hours in the morning when I drive in the park and in the evening when I appear at my chosen entertainments. The rest of the day belongs to you."

It sounded reasonable, but he had no desire to spend that much time in her company. "I didn't think you lacked for escorts."

"Do you know Lady Golpin?"

Gabriel shook his head at the change of topic. "Not that I remember."

"She owns a fantastic diamond necklace. It is enormous. She only wears it if she is accompanied by two armed footmen."

He took a bite of his biscuit and waited. Although he might dislike her methods, he'd begun to suspect that a calculating, logical mind worked inside that beautiful head.

"Everyone is so impressed by the security that no one has thought to question the actual worth of the piece."

"And they should?"

Madeline smiled, a mischievous grin that harkened back to girlhood pranks. "It's paste. She's actually only a stone's throw from losing everything to her creditors."

A matching grin threatened to form on his face until it occurred to him that her smile was likely a ploy calculated to draw that reaction from him. To gain his compliance.

"It is in my best interest to look like I have something worth protecting."

He stilled as another correlation to Lady Golpin occurred to him. "Lady Golpin uses this tactic to hide the truth. Are you doing the same thing?"

Would she admit it?

"Are you asking me if I'm a virgin?" She looked thoroughly entertained by the question. "Why do you care, Mr. Huntford?"

Gabriel placed the biscuit on his plate. He didn't care, yet he found himself leaning forward. "I think I should know the value of the commodity I'm protecting."

"Immense, of course." She blew gently on her cup of tea.

Tiny pinpricks covered his arms as his body reacted to the imagined sensation of that air moving over his skin. "It's my reputation you're hiring as well as my skills. Are you a virgin?"

She sipped her drink and swallowed, sending a ripple down her throat. "What else could I be?"

"Very clever or foolish. Are you truly untouched?"

The sparkle in her eyes dimmed, and she returned her cup to the tray. "I never claimed that. If you want further assurance, you'll have to bid on me yourself." She rose to her feet. "Now I also must be clear that I have several rules I will insist upon. First, all information you discover will be reported to me, no matter how insignificant it might seem."

Gabriel nodded. He'd give her any information that might affect her auction. He would not be telling her, however, about his own private inquiry. He'd do everything she'd hired him for. If he chose to do more, that was his business. He quelled a stab of guilt. He hadn't lured his suspects into bidding on her. With or without his involvement, they'd still be pursuing her. In fact, she was safer because of him.

"Next, your investigation into my bidders' private lives remains private. I won't risk scaring potential bidders away."

That suited his purposes perfectly. "Anything else?"

"One last thing. Your only payment will be monetary. Under no circumstances will I sleep with you or pleasure you in any way." Her gaze swept over him, lingering on his lower body. "No matter the size of the bulge in your trousers. Are we agreed?"

Resisting the urge to look down, Gabriel gave a curt nod. "I'm at your service."

ABOUT THE AUTHOR

ANNA RANDOL lives and writes in sunny Southern California. When she's not plotting sexy storylines, she's usually eating chocolate, having wild dance parties with her kids in the living room, or remodeling her house, one ill-planned project at a time. Anna loves to hear from her readers through her website at www.annarandol.com or on Twitter @AnnaRandol.

Be Impulsive!

Look for Other
Avon Impulse Authors

www.AvonImpulse.com